Leslie was born in a small village and lived in the pleasant, wooded countryside. From an early age, he worked on a village farm, and he has always been associated with different forms of transport. He has always loved writing and, now he is retired, spends a lot of his time doing so for others to enjoy, and is now settled into a writing career.

The book is dedicated to all those, of any age, who can believe that the little folk are about, and their involvement in our everyday life is more than just a pleasant thought. With an easy introduction to the Scottish Gaelic, and a wish for you to meet and enjoy a time with Duncan and Isabella McTreggle, Gnelfs of Scotland.

Leslie H. Harvey

THE GNELFS OF SCOTLAND

AUSTIN MACAULEY PUBLISHERS®

LONDON * CAMBRIDGE * NEW YORK * SHARJAH

A CIP catalogue record for this title is available from the British Library.

ISBN 9781035886937 (Paperback)
ISBN 9781035886944 (ePub e-book)

www.austinmacauley.com

First Published 2025
Austin Macauley Publishers Ltd®
1 Canada Square
Canary Wharf
London
E14 5AA

Jessica Adams

Margeret Withers

Paul Withers

John Wakefield

My sincere thanks to my many friends who inadvertently guided me.

Table of Contents

Introduction

The story begins with a gnome boy and an elf girl who go against all accepted traditions and are married on the Isle of Arran in the Gaelic south.

It is this marriage that has come to be recognised as the beginning of a new gnelf population many distances away from Arran, near the town of Steornabhagh (Stornoway) on the Isle of Leodhais (Lewis) on the Western Isles of Scotland, in the Gaelic north, out in the Sea of the West.

This is a version from the Gaelic of the story of the gnelfs according to Duncan McTreggle, the First Gnelf Elder of Steornabhagh, and many consider it to be the first story in the history of the Gnelfs of Scotland.

I hereby bid you welcome to the Gaelic world, where truth and kindness go hand in hand.

Leslie H. Harvey of Kimberley.

A h-uile la sona dhuibh's gun la idir dona dhuibh.
(*Uh hooluh lah sonnuh ghuh-eev skoon laheejir*
donnuh ghuh-eev.)
May all your days be happy ones.

In the Beginning

The Story of the Hermit of Tirindrish.

Told of the hermit by Gnelf Elder Duncan Dunky McTreggle, and translated from the Gaelic:

Some time ago, I met an old Man of the Highlands, an elderly man who was wearing an old grey kilt and a soft scruffy dark blue woolly cap. He had a folded grey blanket over his shoulder, and he was gripping a long wooden staff; one that seemed to be holding him up, for he was older than old.

It was a cold rainy morning, and I had just celebrated my 20th birthday the day before, so, I was a wee bit muggle-minded.

The old man had bid me sit with him for a wee while and listen to his story. I motioned at the rain, but he just shrugged his shoulders, while at the same time loosening the folded blanket, to allow it to fall over his knees as he sat on the branch of a fallen tree.

I sat myself down with the rain pouring over me. I still wonder at this, as he talked the rain ceased, and the sun began to shine on the two of us there in the forest.

It was as if we were deserving of its true warmth; a consideration much like the warmth a body can often get after drinking a hot sweet cup of tea.

The old man told me of his first day in the forest. It was strange, but as he talked, I could somehow sense the passing of years, as if I was travelling through time with him.

He told me of his memory of a battle fought bravely by many of his fellow compatriots, but it was a battle they lost.

However, he was sure that their loss on that day was much more than losing a fight or a battle. From what he told me, it would seem that his life changed from that sad day; with him deciding to live alone in the wilds of the Scottish glens and hills, where he had become content in remembering what had once been. But at the same time knowing in his heart that the old life had gone forever.

The old man spoke in a whisper that had the lilt of Gaelic.

The hermit spoke sharp, but gently, and I made a new friend.

Duncan McTreggle

Chapter 1
Banishment

To the south of Glasgow, on the Isle of Arran in the Firth of Clyde, there is the calm leafy world of an old forest that took its name from the nearby little town of Blackwaterfoot.

It was in this forest, in the year 2000, that a gnome and an elf of an old forest family fell in love. Even though they were of a different race and clan, they wished to be married.

The young little chap in question was a gnome called Duncan Treggle. He was, at around 15 centimetres in height, a wee bit small for a gnome, and the young little lady he was in love with was an elf girl. One by the name of Isabella Papplewick, and at the same 15 centimetres in height, she was suitably tall for an elf.

To all the other little folk who lived in the forest, this proposed marriage was a serious matter indeed. The one that went against all known rules and the set of laws of the gnome and elf world and a meeting of the Elders was called for.

The item on the agenda.
The proposed marriage of Duncan Treggle, a gnome of the Forest of
Blackwaterfoot, and Isabella Papplewick, an elf of the Forest of
Blackwaterfoot.

After much discussion, the gnome and elf Elders of the forest folk did in due course kindly agree to the mixed marriage. It was maybe the first, but it would not be the last.

However, after they were married, the young couple upset things even more, by calmly stating that it was their intention to live above ground in

Blackwaterfoot Forest, an area of gnome and elf land where living underground was the only accepted way.

This proposal to live above ground was another serious matter indeed, and another meeting of the Elders was called.

The item on the agenda.
Duncan Treggle's and Isabella Papplewick's proposal to live above ground.

However, this time the Elders were shocked, it was not right and proper for gnomes and elves to live above ground; not when living below ground had been the birthright of all gnomes and elves for thousands of time-years. It just would not do, and the proposal could not be accepted.

More meetings took place between the couple and their own families and the Elders, but the young newlyweds would not budge. They had the notion to be free and live where and how they pleased, and as far as they were concerned, if they so wished they could live above ground in some old tree, and not stop to think or bother about any silly rules.

Time went by, and Duncan and Isabella gave up on the tree idea and lived in a cave while they tried again, and again, to get the Elders to agree to their living above ground. In a state of tizzy, although not full panic, the gnome and elf Elders held more meetings and discussed the out-of-the-ordinary application from the young couple.

Then they came to the only decision possible:

"It was not right for a gnome or an elf to live above the ground in the Forest of Blackwaterfoot when living under it was something that the gnomes and elves of the forest had done for many more time-years than that could be counted."

As you might expect, after calming down, and perhaps, unhappily so, the Elders had another meeting.

The item on the agenda.
The banishment of Duncan Treggle and Isabella Treggle.

As far as the Elders could see it, if Mr Duncan Treggle and Mrs Isabella Treggle were determined to live above ground, they would have to leave the world of Blackwaterfoot Forest, and the Isle of Arran to do so, to confirm this decision, they made a lasting and official declaration.

Declaration:

It is hereby decreed by the Elders of Blackwaterfoot Forest, Duncan Treggle and Isabella Treggle must leave Blackwaterfoot Forest and the Isle of Arran, and go to the north, to the Isle of Leodhais (Lewis) out in the West.

It had not been an easy decision to make, but the Elders of Blackwaterfoot Forest knew that they had to keep their underground world a safe secret, and move away from those who wanted to live above ground, move them a long way away.

Even though the young couple and their families and friends protested, and more meetings were held, the two newlyweds were, in due course, made to leave. They were told again that they must go and find a new home for themselves in the far-off place of Stcornabhagh (Stornoway); a harbour town on the western Isle of Leodhais (Lewis)—and never return to Blackwaterfoot Forest and the Isle of Arran.

The two newlyweds were given no choice but to emigrate; to leave the Isle of Arran and make their way across hills and glens, and water to the Western Isles of Scotland.

Author's Note:

Like all fairy folk, gnelfs can live for hundreds of time-years, and all gentlemen gnelfs boast a white beard and a moustache from about the age of 10. However, they do stay young and childlike until they are two to three hundred years of age.

The lady gnelfs also live for hundreds of time-years, but they are more serious and are always making sure that all is right with them and their family.

Chapter 2
Gnelfs and Emigrating

It was a calm fine morning of mist and sunshine, and the newly married gnelfs, Mr and Mrs Treggle, were on the Isle of Arran; standing together on the top of a small cliff above the shore of the Kilbrannan Sound, a stretch of water between the Isle of Arran and the mainland of the Kintyre.

Although it was a view they would always remember. But sadly, it was a view they would never see again.

They stood in the shadows cast by the hills behind them, with the waters to their front glistening with bright early morning light.

They knew they would soon be crossing those same bright waters on their long journey to their new home on the island of Leodhais, far off in the Sea of the West.

First, they had to make their way along the west coast of Arran, to the little port of Lochranza in the north of the island, where their journey to a new life together would really begin.

After saying their tearful goodbyes to the rest of their families, the two, who from then on, would be known not as elf or gnome but as gnelf, set forth walking along at a very slow pace by the A841 road of traffic to Tormore, the next village to the north.

Duncan put his arm around his wife, lovingly pulling her closer to him, and as they stood together for a moment, he tried to catch or wipe her tears, using a small bunch of heather flower heads he was managing to hold in his free hand. He thought he needed to comfort her.

However, his pretty wife's response was not what he expected.

"Get away, yer silly wee man!" She wriggled away from him as she spoke, with her voice sounding like the sharp tones of a small bell in the clear morning air, the mist had lifted. "What are you trying to do with that flower bunch? Are you looking to see if I have a liking for heather butter?"

But then, she seemed to relax a wee bit, as if she was having a second thought. Maybe even thinking that, perhaps, it was not *his* fault alone that she was standing where she was.

Then she had a third thought, thinking that she should try to get her new husband to wake up to the new reality, and maybe understand the true meaning of the situation they were in. With this in mind, she spoke to him in a voice a bit more on the tinkly mellow side of a tone.

"Come on, Dunky, we haven't got time-flicks to mess about with the heather flowers. We've got to find somewhere to live! A new home is more important than heather butter!" The little gnelf lady paused as she looked back up the hill towards the forest that had once been her home world. "And we aren't going back, that's for sure! They will not let us; we are *emgrants* (emigrants) now."

The heather flower bunch that Duncan was holding fell to the ground. He looked just a wee bit sad as the petals and stems fell out of his hand, tumbling like a cluster of tiny green-blue and purple butterflies.

He could sense that Isabella was upset, and he spoke to her as nicely as he could, "You are right, my dear one, but there wer' no need for you to be snappy with me. You have always said as how you wanted to live above ground in the fresh air with me." He paused for a flick or two and then continued, his voice a little deeper, "You said, it would be good for the *pàisdean* (little children), an' you said as how you trusted me. So, why are you getting uppity with me, eh?"

He had been holding his wife's hand when he had come to the end of his question; and his dear little wife had pulled him close, to give her answer by ruffling her face in his soft white beard and the floppy front of his green jacket sort of thing.

Then, she laughed in a chuckling kind of fashion and told him not to be so daft. Of course, she had promised to live with him above ground, and she wasn't worried. (Gnelfs don't actually worry anyway, although they do sometimes get a bit bothered, or *tizzicky*) In truth, she was proud of the fact that from then on, they would be known as gnelfs.

"I am not getting uppity, and I am proud to say that you an' me are the first gnelfs, ever."

Author's Note:

19

Isabella was wrong in that assumption.

Isabella said the words in a voice that had taken on a sort of noble way of speaking, but then it softened slightly, and Duncan could feel her arms tightening around him as she said that no matter what they were going to be, *they would always be together.*

Walking for some flicks of time, they came to a bridge over Machriewater, a gentle clear stream that ran from the mountains of Arran to Machrie Bay, and Duncan spotted a road sign pointing in the direction of Machrie, over a track that looked to be not much more than a footpath.

"Should we go that way, Izzy?" A simple question, if truth be told, but it was their first real decision on which path to take, and neither of them had a clue.

However, Isabella was more thoughtful and a wee bit more intelligent than lady gnelfs usually are.

"No, I don't think we should. It would be better if we keep by the waters and follow the shore 'till we find a place to cross."

It was a logical thing to say, but what she did not, or could not know was that there would be no way to cross the waters of the sound, apart from the Cal Mac ferry, the little MV Loch Tarbert.

As they walked on, they came to a flow of spring water near The Schoolhouse by the road to Lochranza. It was water that was so fresh, cold and clear, that to watch it gurgling out of the grassy hillside as it did between a smooth jumble of mossy stones, was to wonder at Mother Nature's cleverness at providing such a plentiful supply of good, sweet and healthy drinking water for free.

With the green soft moss on the stones making a soft cushion, for a gnelf that is, they thought it a good place to stop and rest for a while.

They rested gladly, content to watch and listen to the clear water rippling over the many stones and pebbles in the stream. After their rest, they later make their way below a group of ancient standing stones near Lorsa Water. It was a beautiful spot, but they needed to get on. So, they continued to make their slow way along the A841 road of traffic to the next little place, a settlement called Imachar.

"We should stop now, Izzy. We need to eat."

Of course, what Dunky really meant to say was that he was hungry.

They looked around for food, and found a good supply of buttercups and dandelions, and twigs and leaves, enough to make a reasonable teatime tea. It was the first food time of their own as immigrant gnelfs, maybe they would try buttercup salad, with a side touch of dandelion leaves, and perhaps, a few hawthorn green twigs: nice, if you are a gnelf.

Not many time-flicks later, and after having enjoyed a good meal, the two little folks did what most little folk do after a meal…they went to sleep, in a bed they made in the long grass.

They were in a small wood of not many trees between the road of traffic and the waters, and it was there they stayed until the following day, their first full day on their own as gnelfs proper.

Ciamar a gheibh mi ann?

Kimmer uh yaev mee a-oo<u>n</u>?

How can I get there?

Chapter 3
Float-Walking, and a Ride on the Lochranza-Claonaig Ferry

Even though Isabella had always known that gnomes and elves could float-walk. She could not do it, and she had never seen her husband Duncan do it either. She had been amazed when on the morning of the second day, just as the early mist was rising and the dew on the grass was beginning to dry, he did his float-walking along the path down to the *seashore*, where the ground levelled out.

She asked her question in a certain emergency way, "You never told me you could do that?"

(He did not know he could float-walk either)

It was a surprised Duncan who answered his elf wife, and now gnelf, "I didn't know I could 'til…until just then, Izzy. It just sort of happened!"

Then, taking things in hand, Duncan stood perfectly still and took a couple of intakes of air.

Holding his hands easily by his sides, he breathed in again, and with a surprised look on his face, he gently lifted off the sandy path and started to float-walk along towards the water. It just felt like the natural thing to do…It was very easy. All he did was breathe in some air and hold his breath.

He turned to look back, pleadingly at his wife and dropped slightly as he spoke, "Why don't you try it, Izzy?"

Isabella shook her head at her floating husband. "Don't be daft, what would I want with floating around like that, I'd look silly!"

Mrs Isabella Treggle was not the sort of gnelf lady who took chances, even when her husband said, "It'll be fine. There is only me here, Izzy, an' I dunna think you will look daft at all. Go on, have a go."

Not too sure if she could do it, a nervous Isabella took a quick extra intake of air and then gave out with a low murmured *oops* as her feet left the ground.

Then, she flopped back down again, with her hands brushing the bottom of her skirt away from the danger of lodging against any grass or boulders, or heaps of sand. She then stood as she was before, with her feet settled on the soft sandy ground in amongst the bits of dewy grasses.

Needless to say, Isabella's attempt at float-walking had made her feel a wee bit hot and bothered; she had not done it before, and as far as she was concerned it didn't seem right at all, not natural, and she was not in too much of a hurry to try float-walking again, if ever again at all!

However, her husband had other ideas. "Go on, *Izzy*! That wa' good. Go on! Try again."

It would seem that the young husband was keen for his young wife to learn how to float-walk, even though he had not really learned how to do it properly himself. But (to prove a point, I suppose) he took a couple of gulps of air and grabbed hold of the thin end of a conveniently placed low-hanging branch of a nearby bush as he did so. Then, full of breath in the air, he floated himself up to a level height, roughly speaking, and bobbed about a bit.

Then, by keeping his breathing to a controlled slow in and out, he managed to keep himself more or less in a steady position, with his knees brushing against the dew-covered grass tops.

He smiled nicely at his wife, and smugly said, "Look, Izzy, it's sae easy."

Looking carefully at her floating husband, Isabella threw caution to the wind, took two lady-like gulps of air, and lifted smoothly off the ground.

This time she managed to rise just above the grass, boulders, sand and weeds quite delicately, with her arms held stiffly down her sides, her wrists seemingly glued to the top of her legs through her skirt, while her hands flapped rapidly in short fluttering bursts.

She then blew out her breath in one long and easy blow and dropped daintily and expertly to the weed and grass-covered sandy ground—thinking as she did so that she was doing what the fairies do so nicely, and making it look to be easy.

Smiling at Isabella's dainty performance and being more certain of his own skills in the float-walking technique, Duncan let go of his grip on the thin branch and grasses he had been using to steady himself. He then leaned slightly against the light breeze coming off the land to the waters, and by doing so he was able to gently sway himself to a slow float-walk that he could sort of control.

Isabella watched her husband moving along just above the weeds and grass, and she seemed to take courage from his renewed and determined efforts.

Placing her arms firmly down her sides again, she took a couple of intakes of air; not too much mind, and lifted gracefully off the ground, with her hands fluttering in quick bursts of action, in order to keep her balance. This way, she followed her floating husband towards the road to the next hamlet of Whitefarland.

Although the two of them were absolute beginners, and far from being fully skilled, they were able to gently float-walk along the road of traffic at what was something a wee bit faster than the normal gnelf walking pace; with their feet touching the tops of the wispy blades of grass here and there.

Sometime later, the two of them stood on the road of traffic itself, just across from a hotel at Catacol, looking out across the water that was such a huge expanse of a barrier they did not know how they were going to cross.

Isabella put the problem into words, "How are we going to get across such big waters?"

Duncan gave the matter some thought and then, prepared to make a suggestion.

However, before he could do so, a barking sort of voice from behind and above them asked a couple of questions, "What are you two doing standing there, eh? You're not thinking of swimming, are you?"

It was Coyrie, a black and white lady collie dog of some great age (for dogs that is) who was asking the questions.

Author's Note:

If I have not mentioned this before, I will mention it now. Gnelfs can talk with all creatures and plants, and that includes collie dogs, and folk like you and me, of course. They use the Gaelic but can talk in any language.

Duncan and Isabella looked up and around, while Isabella asked a question of her own, "What is *swimming?*"

Coyrie gave a low growl of a laugh and said, "It's nae matter, you will not do it, you are tae small."

She sat back on her back legs, curled the white tip of her tail around her front legs, and asked another question before either of the two gnelfs could ask another one of their own, "Why are you looking at the water?"

Duncan remained calm and gave a direct answer that made the dog sit up a wee bit higher, "We are off to the Isle of Leodhais, and we know we have to cross the wide waters to get there. We have to follow the setting sun."

Coyrie crossed the road slowly and then lowered herself by placing her front legs further out towards the two gnelfs in front of her, in a one-step-at-a-time movement, and putting her chin on her front paws.

She then asked another question but in a much kinder voice, "Have you been made to leave your home?"

Coyrie was old enough to know that little folk do not go wandering for no reason.

Duncan told the collie their story of having been made to go into exile from the Blackwaterfoot Forest, and that they were now in search of a new home, one they had been told would be waiting for them in Steornabhagh on the Isle of Leodhais out in the west, on the big sea waters.

The old collie dog looked at the two gnelfs, and out at the water between Lochranza and the shore of the Kintyre.

She then lifted her chin from her front paws and spoke softly, her lips hardly moving, "My old granddad used to tell me of how, many years ago, human folk; and *his* long-ago granddad and grandma collie dogs, were made to leave the Isle of Leodhais, and other isles, so that sheep could live there, and now you want to go there?"

She paused for a few flicks of time. "It is a nice thing that you're wantin' to go to our old homeland, and I will do as much as I can to help you…But you will have to remember, it is a long, long way, and there are many hills and waters to cross."

The collie lifted her head and body and sniffed the air, but remained seated on her back legs, with her black, white-tipped tail curling and flicking slightly around her front paws.

Coyrie had been with her master the old ferryman for many years, and she had lived in and around the ferry-point of Lochranza all her life, and she was known by all the folk who lived there.

The kind ferry people and the gentle folk of Lochranza knew Coyrie and were fond of her, and it was with the ferry people's blessing that she often took a ride on the ferry for the 20-minute ride across the waters to the Claonaig Jetty on the mainland of Kintyre.

It was this fact that was running through her doggy mind as her tail flicked in a more rapid movement from side to side, with her head leaning over slightly.

Coyrie had taken a real liking to the two little folks straight away, and when Duncan asked if she could, in fact, help them in their quest to find a new home, the old collie wagged her tail and did not hesitate in saying that she would be happy to help them.

With her tail wagging even faster to show that she had meant what she had said, Coyrie suggested that the two gnelfs should climb into a bag of some sort, and then, let her carry it in her mouth onto the ferry. The three of them would then sit together in a quiet corner on the ferryboat.

Then, on reaching the Claonaig Jetty, on the other side of the water, she would then walk off the boat as she usually did, and carry Duncan and Isabella in the bag until they were far enough away from the jetty where they would be safe on their own.

It was not easy finding a suitable bag; but they did find one, eventually, and even though their choice of bag was a wee bit smelly, they were soon on their way.

Being careful, Coyrie found a nice quiet corner on the passenger deck near the front of the little CalMac ferryboat MV Loch Tarbert, well away from the cars and vans and the passenger folk.

They remained there undisturbed. The ferry people knew Coyrie was there, but were not worried or bothered about her, the only attention being the odd pat on her head from time to time.

The engine of the MV Loch Tarbert began to chug in a mumbling noisy fashion, but in a nice friendly way, and the two gnelfs tried to look out from their hiding place in the bag, but Coyrie pushed them back in the bag with her nose. She then tucked the bag and the gnelfs under her chin with her front paws and snuggled them down with the gentle pressure of her head and chin pushing them in their bag further under the soft white fur on her chest.

Some 20 flicks of time later, after a smooth and pleasant crossing, the ferryboat lightly crunched its way onto the jetty slope, and old Coyrie the collie, walked off carrying her bag in her mouth like a mum carrying a puppy.

Keeping what you might call a low profile, Coyrie weaved her calm way between cars and travelling folk, to arrive at the edge of the heather-strewn moorland of the Kintyre undetected as it were.

Looking around for a moment or two, she found a good spot and let the bag down on the ground. Duncan and Isabella rolled out to make ready for the next stage of their journey, excited in a way, but calm.

Isabella brushed herself down with her hands and thanked the old dog, "Thank you, Coyrie, that was kind of you, and we will always be grateful to you."

Duncan wriggled in his clothes and also said a thank you, and then asked a question, "Can you help us a wee bit further?"

Coyrie woofed a quick answer, "No, I'm sorry, I canna go any further, I've never been further than this, and I have to get the ferry back to Arran...But I will tell you to keep an eye out for Daphne."

Isabella was quick off the mark, "Who is Daphne? What is she?"

Looking carefully back down the sloping ground to the jetty, and keeping an eye on the ferry, Coyrie answered her in a yapping sort of way, "Daphne is a wee deer. She lives in these parts and I am sure she will be able to help you. Just keep going north, that's with the sun on your right shoulder in the morning, and over your left shoulder in the afternoon."

She then made a few yaps of goodbye and ran back down to the jetty to the waiting MV Loch Tarbert, her ears flapping and her tail wagging.

The Gaelic of the gnelfs has an alphabet that consists of 18 letters.
There is no J, K, Q, V, W, X, Y, or Z.
There are five vowels A, E, I, O, U. However, these can be short or long.

Chapter 4
Overland to Oban

The weather remained fair and warm, with hardly any wind to speak of, and Duncan and Isabella made their way north; keeping the sun on their right with it being morning time.

They were float-walking along the tarmac of the road to Claonaig village, the B8001 road that would eventually bring them to the heather and bracken-covered hills of North Kintyre.

Of course, like all creatures, large or small, they did need to stop to eat. After making their way along the road as far as the tiny hamlet of Bruiland, a journey of many flicks of time, they paused by the tinkling waters of a stream.

While they were settled by the water and eating a meal of a few leaves and chewy twigs, Daphne the Deer strolled up quietly and gently, as if on tiptoe, and took a drink right by the gnelfs without saying anything. Then, after taking a slow easy drink, she kept her head low down, looked at Duncan and Isabella and got into chatting with them.

The small deer had a lovely, sweet style of talking as if she was about to sing softly, and Duncan took to her straight away, welcoming her to their mealtime.

"It is lovely to meet with you. You must be Daphne, Coyrie the collie told us about you."

Daphne lifted her head and flicked her ears, and with water dripping off her chin, she spoke to the little gnelf lady, "Oh, hello, my dear, yes I am. Was Coyrie alright? Do you live here? I've not seen you around here before."

Duncan coughed politely, and smiled as he wondered why a deer should call his wife a *deer*? Then, he took it upon himself to answer the deer, "Oh no, we don't live here, we only stopped to have a picnic meal…and Coyrie is fine."

He would have continued, but his dear wife Isabella struck up a conversation with the deer, and he just contented himself by sitting back to listen while chewing on his food.

The little deer listened to the gnelf lady patiently and then tapped her right front foot on the short grass at the side of the road of traffic. "You mustn't stay here too long, it is unsafe. Are you travelling anywhere special, might I ask? Do you know the way?"

The three of them munched at their food for a moment and then Duncan answered, "Well, we are travelling to find a new home."

Daphne the Deer looked up, her ears standing erect. "Oh, so you are immigrants then?"

Isabella was offended, even though she did not really know what an immigrant really was, and Daphne could sense that she had somehow offended the little fairy lady.

With the shame of her comment showing in her expression, the prim little deer tried to say that she did not mean to offend.

"Oh, I'm sorry, I did not mean that immigrants are anything funny or strange."

Duncan stopped chewing for a moment and corrected the deer, "No, we are not *imm'grants*, we are gnelfs, and we are going to the Isle of Leodhais."

Daphne was amazed. "The Isle of Leodhais!" She knew it to be many long distances away. "That is a long way away, even for my friends of Tarbert, and I would think that it would be many more distances away for such little folk like gnelfs."

She lifted her head and looked in the direction of the north, her eyes seeking out the pathway through the trees by the A83 road of traffic to Tarbert.

Isabella said two words quietly, "Oh dear."

As Daphne lowered her head to listen, she chuckled a wee bit and told the little gnelf lady not to be concerned, "I have friends in the forest near Tarbert, and I will take you to them, but you will have to go by my way, and keep off the dangerous road of traffic."

The two gnelfs looked at each other for a moment, and then, Duncan spoke, "We need to get to where we can get on to Leodhais as soon as likely; we need to find our new home—"

Daphne was caring and talked quietly and calmly to her two new friends, "Oh, it's alright, my Dears, I will not hurry without being careful, and our pathways are just a little way off from the road of traffic. Don't worry, they will be smooth and easy, with plenty of food and nice sleeping places. And there will be many friends for you to meet with."

The gnelfs walked and float-walked after Daphne, through the wooded ground near the west side of Loch Fyne, keeping the water of the loch to their right, and the road of traffic to their left all the way. After a long time of walking, they came to a small loch in the hills to the south of Tarbert, a nice calm place where they could rest for a while.

After another short meal of grass and twigs, and after Daphne had failed to find her friends, they turned left to go across the side of the hills until they came to a tall metal mast; which Daphne told the gnelfs was a *mast of signals*, with the little folk none the wiser as to what *sig-nols* were.

Daphne told the two gnelfs to rest and wait for the dark of night. "We will be on the dangerous road of traffic for just a wee while, (the A83), and then, we will go into the forested hills on the other side, and find the Fort of Dunadd, where I know it is safe."

Thankfully, the crossing of the road of traffic was done quickly, and easily, but the journey through the forest in the evening dark was a wee bit on the tricky side for the two gnelfs, owing to the fact that they could not float-walk in the dark. However, thanks to Daphne, who carried them on her back for most of the time, the three of them, eventually, sneaked by the town of Lochgilphead in secret.

Keeping up a steady pace, and following the A816 road of traffic to Oban, they arrived on the very top of the heather and bracken-covered hills, and at the Fort of Dunadd before the real dark of night could begin.

When the real darkness did arrive, and the cold of the night began to bite, Daphne curled up in a hollow by a wall of the fort out of the cold night wind, and with Duncan and Isabella curling up close to the deer's warm tummy, the three of them made it through the night dark, comfortably and peacefully.

The morning came with its damp cool air, making the grassy and mossy ground wet and clingy to the feet of the two gnelfs. Sadly, their soft shoes did nothing to stop the wet drenching through to their feet; living in the forest had meant that dewy grass was never a problem. Now, they were out in the open, it was another story and an uncomfortable one at that.

However, Daphne came to the rescue again, and for the journey down through the heather to the flowing waters of the Abhainn na Guile, they walked up by the stream and kept to the quiet Glen of Chaorainn until they came to the loch of the same name.

After a brief rest, the deer and her two little friends began to make their way north, going steadily and carefully by the busy A816 road of traffic, and with the sun now over on their right, the two little gnelfs became aware of a weird feeling coming over them as they walked.

Daphne sensed their concern and tried to put their minds at rest, "We are going through between the rise of the Cruach Gille Bheagain on our left and the rise of the Cruach Chaorainn on our right. I have been this way many times, and I know there is nothing to fear."

Eventually, they came to a trail that took them around to the north of the hill of Gille Bheagain and through the trees to the north. It was a long winding trail, but it seemed to be a quiet and safe one, and three friends made steady progress in the cooling fresh morning air of the forest. The scent of the pines made it a nice journey for the two little gnelfs, it reminded them of their old home on the Isle of Arran in the Forest Blackwaterfoot.

Some flicks of time went by as they followed the trail through the trees, and then the three travellers, eventually, came to the edge of the forest, and out onto the huge expanse of the hilly land between Glen Feochan and Glen Lonan.

While they had been in amongst the trees of the forest, there had been some protection from much of the wild weather. But out in the open, in the mist and murk of a rainy afternoon, it was not so good, and it was a concerned Duncan who asked Daphne the Deer if they were on the true path to Oban.

Daphne was not too sure, but she did try to make the little gnelf feel at ease, "Well, Dunky, I do not know the true path as you call it. I have only been here once, and that was when I was a youngster with my mother some time ago." She looked out through the mist. "All the same, I can remember that some of my mother's friends live around here somewhere. All we need do is wait until one of them finds us."

However, Isabella did not think the dear deer was right about waiting. "Would it not be better if we go look for them? Could we not just keep going to the north?"

Daphne the Deer snorted politely; her nostrils were filling with the cold mist. "Yes, I suppose we could carry on, for a little way. But not too far, mind, we could quite easily get lost, and then, what would we do?"

Isabella was sweet and sharp with her answer, "We could wait for your friends to find us."

Daphne chuckled. "Yes, I suppose we might as well be found lost as wait to be found here."

Author's Note:

I still have not worked that one out yet.

The three of them set off across the wild open space of the highland of the Oban hills. Even though it was misty and cold to the bones, Duncan and Isabella were able to stay cheerful, singing an old song that Duncan had learned as a young gnome.

> *We don't know if we go too slow.*
> *We don't know if we can dare.*
> *But we do know that if we go,*
> *We will nicely get there.*

Daphne trotted on in time with the song, with her head swinging from one side to the other, and she was soon joined by the two gnelfs, who jumped and float-walked in time to the singing.

They had sung the little rhyme over and over for about 10 times when just ahead of them, standing on a rock, was Esknish the Stag. He was huge, a real giant of a stag deer, with his antlers, although not fully developed, spreading on either side of his lofty and proud head.

Duncan and Isabella held themselves in check when Esknish spoke, the two of them in a grumpy voice, as they tried to hide in the heather behind their friend Daphne the Deer, "I am Esknish, who might your three be, and where might ye be going?"

Duncan poked his head up out of the heather. "I am Duncan Treggle, and this is Isabella, my wife, and this is Daphne the Deer, our true friend. And we might be…we are going to the Isle of Leodhais, to find—"

Esknish the Stag interrupted, "But you are many distances from the Magic Isle, and it is far across the big waters—" Duncan made as if to speak again, but the stag carried on, "There are not many trees on that far distant Isle, and there are no other gnomes like you as far as I know, but I could be wrong…But it is a Magic Isle. Why would—"

It was Isabella's turn to interrupt, "We are not gnomes, we are gnelfs, and we are going to the *Magic Isle* of Leodhais to start a new life together." She stood as tall as she could, her head and shoulders just above the heather flowers. "If there are no other gnomes, elves or gnelfs on the island, then we will be the first." She paused for a few flicks of time. "And we will be the magic!"

The quiet that followed was a sweet kind of quiet, and the mist drifted hither and thither as silence reigned between the stag and the three friends.

Then Esknish spoke to Daphne, his voice slightly softer, "Why do *you* wish to go to the western Isle of Leodhais, my dear deer, there are no creatures like us on that island?" The big stag thought for a flick or two and then spoke again, "Or is there?"

Daphne was polite, and she moved up closer to the stag to talk with him in a whisper, "I will not be going with them. I am only trying to help them on their way…I will be returning to my own forest on the Kintyre when I leave them at Oban."

She looked at Esknish carefully. "I am sure there will be creatures like us on the island, yes, I am sure there will be."

Duncan and Isabella did hear what Daphne and Esknish whispered, but neither of them thought it proper to interfere.

Esknish spoke again, "I think you are both foolish, but if that is what you want to do, I will see if I can guide you for part of the way…Come with me, and do not delay."

The big stag gruffly whispered goodbye to Daphne and turned to walk away, and Duncan and Isabella only had time to shout goodbye to Daphne as they struggled to follow the big stag as he walked off into the thickening mist.

Moving along with Daphne the Deer had been very easy; she had even carried them for a long part of the way. But Esknish the Stag was different, if he carried anything it was his head, held high above his massive shoulders.

Trying to keep up, Duncan fell over for the umpteenth time. He sat up and shouted at Esknish the Stag, "Double dash this for a game of mushrooms, *(I am not sure what he meant)* I am not following you one step further. It is alright for you to stride out and push your way through the bracken, but me and Izzy can't do that, we are too small."

Esknish looked down at the little gnelf. "Ah but, my little friend, I canna do anything about that, but if you use your tiny brain for a moment, you might work out how to—"

Isabella interrupted, "You mean we have other ways to move along that might help us to stay with you?"

Esknish coughed a slight cough and then, lifted his right front leg as high as it would go. He then lifted his front left leg to the same loftiness, and the front of his huge body lifted up. He then lifted his two back legs and floated off into the mist, coughing in a laugh as he went.

The two gnelfs looked at each other when, from out of the mist, they heard the big stag shout, "Come on you two, just do it, no messin', just do it."

Duncan lifted his right leg as high as he could get, *(which wasn't very high, really)* and he then lifted his left leg as high as he could and floated off into the mist.

Isabella was astonished. Her husband and a big daft stag had just floated off into the mist and were nowhere to be seen.

Then, before she could think of shouting for him, her missing husband shouted from out of the mist, "Do it *Izzy*, just do it."

Author's Note:

It did take some believing at first when Duncan told me of their flight *to Oban, but I did conclude that it must have been as he said. Ah, but then, have you ever seen a stag in full flight?*

Their arrival in Oban was not seen by anyone, which I suppose was mainly because they *landed* behind the McGaig's Tower up on the hills above the town, late on a misty evening, and well away from any prying human eyes.

Esknish asked the two gnelfs if they knew what they would be doing next, and Duncan quickly pointed out that they had been told that they must journey to the Isle of Leodhais to make their new home, and that is what they would do.

The stag looked at the two gnelfs, snorted politely, and stamped his front right foot on the hard turf. "You may have been told that, my little friend, but do you know how you are going to get there? I have brought you to Oban, but I canna take you any further…I must bid you goodbye here and be on my way back to the hills, and the heather of the mountains and glens of Argyll, it is where I belong."

He turned to look out across the Bay of Oban. "I wish you a safe journey, my little friends, but I know I must say my farewell."

The big stag shuffled on his four legs and then did a quick about turn and moved gracefully off into the mist and the trees.

Isabella shouted goodbye to Esknish the Stag and then, spoke to her little husband Duncan, "Right then, Dunky, here we are, what do we do next, eh?"

Duncan had not got a clue really, and he just smiled nicely and said the first thing that came into his mind; which was that their resting place was too much in the open and that they should retreat into the nearby trees to seek out their next meal.

The little gnelf lady took a look around and then agreed but said that she needed to sleep more than eat. Within a couple of flicks of time she relaxed to the point where she could not help but close her eyes, and take a sleep-nap, right there by the tower.

Meanwhile, shrugging his shoulders, Duncan felt the need to explore, and within not too many flicks of time after Isabella had gone to sleep, he float-walked over to a fallen tree.

Author's Note:

Duncan uses the term Squig, *meaning* Squirrel. *I thought it best to use the name Squirrel; I hope that you can agree.*

Anyway, Squirrel *goes better with* Cyril. *It will maybe change to* Squig *later in the story.*

Cyril the Squirrel (Squig) was a young red squirrel who had come across gnomes and elves before. But when a little gnelf poked his head over and around the roots of the fallen tree he was sitting on, Cyril whooped in surprise; a sound that was something like a cross between a spit and a whistle.

Duncan drew back, and Cyril the Squirrel hopped up to the little gnelf and asked a question, "Hello, who are you?"

Duncan calmly replied, "I am Duncan Treggle, and I am a gnelf."

Cyril was confused. "No, you are not, you are a gnome."

Duncan agreed. "Yes, you are right, but I am a gnome who has become a gnelf. And my wife is an elf who has become a gnelf." He paused for a flick of time. "And we gnelfs are on a long journey to the island of Leodhais, where we will make our new home."

Duncan told the squirrel of his and his wife Isabella's desire to live above ground. He also told the twitchety squig of how the Elders of the gnome and elf clan Elders on the Island of Arran had made a decree, that he and his wife should leave Arran and find the island of Leodhais, and the town of Steornabhagh, and live above ground there.

Cyril the Squirrel sat up and looked Duncan straight in the eye. "I have lived above ground all my life, and it is grand, and there are other creatures here that live below ground…We all live a happy life here…Why don't you and your elf wife stay here and live with us?"

Duncan could see the sense in what the squig was saying, but he had to be honest and tell him that a gnome/elf decree must be obeyed, and to the letter. Even if he and Isabella did want to settle by the loch, the gnome and elf Elders on Arran would find out about their not obeying the decree, and the punishment would be severe.

Cyril looked away into the trees and spoke quietly, "I do understand about others watching you and wanting to do you harm, we have grey squirrels, who live on the other side of the hills, and they would want us red squirrels to go away and live somewhere else, but we have always lived here, and we want to stay."

Duncan sat by the little red squig and asked a question, "Have they made any decrees?"

The little squirrel twitched and twittered, flicking his bushy tail sharply. "No decree can make us move…and even if they made a decree, why should we obey it, eh?"

The gnelf could not understand this. *a decree once made had to be obeyed*, that was the way of things, in the gnome and elf world at anyway, and now in the new gnelf world, it would seem.

While Duncan was thinking of what the red squig had said, the same *squirrel* asked him if he was fine.

He answered Cyril the Squirrel cheerfully, "Of course, I'm fine!"

The squig asked again. "What would it be if you were not so fine, eh?"

Duncan looked at the squig. The little gnelf was confused, although he had never felt better. "I am not, *not so fine*. I am really very fine, indeed."

Cyril interrupted, "Ah but, you might think you are very fine, but actually, you are not so fine… If you think of the journey, you are on, and how far you still have to go, you should think yourself to be not so fine."

Duncan wondered for a few flicks of time and then asked Cyril the Squirrel about something that bothered him, "If I am not so fine because of the journey we are on, how far is it we still have to travel then?"

The squirrel jumped up on the old tree stump and twitchy twitched as he gave Duncan the news, "You have to go over many hills and cross many streams of water, and lochs and big sea waters…I keep myself to my little world this side of the hills, and the grey squirrels keep to the other side of the hills."

The squirrel thought for a flick of time or two. "But I do know that Obbity Owl and his brother Orchy, the Eagle Owls of Argyll, have often said that the Western Isles are a long, long, long way away over hills streams, lochs, and seas. They have flown high into the sky and seen over the hills to the lochs and seas.

"And they did say that the only island they could see was not even the one of the wests where you are going to, and even that was many days of travel away, even for them on their wings."

Duncan stood up to his full height, with his eyes level with the squig's front paws. "Who are Obbity and Orchy the Owls then? Where are they? I would like to have a word with them, they might know the best way for Isabella and me to go."

After twitching his tail a few times, and scurrying up and down the nearest tree, Cyril the Squirrel told Duncan how to find Obbity and Orchy, and Duncan went to wake Isabella to tell her the news. "We need to find an owl."

Isabella rubbed her eyes and sat up. "What do we need to find an *anowl* for? And what or who is an *anowl*?"

Duncan looked around before answering his little wife, "Not *anowl*, an owl, one by the name of Obbity, and one by the name of Orchy."

The little gnelf lady was not amused, in fact, she was a wee bit huffy at her husband. She had been having a wonderful dream about being in a nice new home, in a woodland full of flowers and other happy creatures like herself and Duncan, and he had disturbed her dream.

"And what will these magic *owls* do for us, eh? Can an owl make dreams come true, eh?"

Duncan was getting confused. "What dreams?"

His little wife spoke on further. "If your Obbity and Orchy are clever owls, why are we sitting here talking?"

Duncan was more confused. He was standing, and who had said anything about Obbity and Orchy being clever and would know the secrets of dreams?

At that moment, Cyril the Squirrel scampered over to the gnelfs, and, after saying hello to Isabella, he told them how to find Obbity and Orchy by walking into the trees and then listening for the *oot-oot*.

The only snag with Cyril's help was that he was a squirrel, and the nearest he could get to an *oot-oot* was *tchoot-tchoot*. it wasn't until Duncan and Isabella did have the real experience of hearing Obbity and his brother Orchy, that they knew the difference between *tchoot-tchoot* and *oot-oot*.

S e obair là tòiseachadh
(Sheh oebir lah tawshochugh)
It's a day's work to get started.

Chapter 5
The Obbity and Orchy Way

Obbity and Orchy were very large eagle owls, but they were at the same time kind and understanding eagle owls; even though they were much more eagle than owl. Even so, they were very calm in the kindest of ways to the two little travellers, but Isabella did think that the owls did look a wee bit fierce.

All the same, within a few flicks of time, Obbity and Orchy had made it clear that without doubt, the two little gnelfs would need their help if they were to make it to the Isle of Leodhais.

Eagle owls really are very large bird-giants of owls with huge wings, and fortunately, that did mean that it was easy for Obbity and Orchy to carry the two gnelfs on their back. Which is what they would have to do if they were going to help the two wanderers; and hanging from the owls' clawed feet would not have been very comfortable or safe for the little folk.

Although Isabella was very nervous about flying on an owl's back, she did, eventually, sit on Obbity's broad back, while her husband Duncan sat on Orchy's back.

Clinging on to tufty feathers in the tightest of tight grips, Duncan and Isabella Treggle then flew with Obbity and Orchy over the hills and glens of the uplands of Argyll and Bute, and away from the harbour town of Oban.

For a good many flicks of time, they flew over the land in an easy passage in the cooling, dry and calm air, with the two owls falling slowly to check their position, and then rising steadily again, to gain some more distance as they glided along on their huge wings.

Duncan and Isabella were a wee bit uncertain at first, they had float-walked before and took flight in the mist with a stag, but this was different. They were a long way up from the ground on the backs of Obbity and Orchy, and it was getting dark; and if they did happen to fall off?

However, thankfully, they did not fall off, their way was easy, and it did even become easier as the giant owls glided along the glens, their huge wings hardly moving.

Then, after covering over 20 distances, and with a few flaps of their wings, Obbity and Orchy lifted far above the Forest of Barcaldine, and then over Loch Creran, to the land by the Stream of Salachan, in the glen of the same name.

After a good rest, the owls took the two gnelfs onwards, and the dark hills and glens seemed to pass underneath them in quick succession as they flew further and further north, and nearer and nearer the gnelfs' new homeland of Leodhais.

From the soft feathery back of the owls, Duncan and Isabella could look down from time to time and see the many castles that Scotland was famous for; with their shadowy grey walled structures looking like *toys* from their lofty travelling. It was a view of the Scotland-world they would ever forget.

Author's Note:

If you have ever seen the Western Isles of Scotland on a warm misty day, I am sure you must have experienced the comforting and mind-settling view of those mist-covered islands out on the lochs, and out to sea. That, my dear reader, is what greeted our two gnelfs as they were carried further and further to the north and west. If you can see that view in your mind's eye now, you are at one with the gnelfs of Leodhais and Scotland.

After nearly another 20 distances, and with the sun of a new day coming up over to their right, Obbity and Orchy decided that they needed to rest, along with, perhaps, something to eat, and the two gnelfs found themselves back on the ground again.

They had landed at a place called Signal Rock in Glencoe, with the river at their side, the hill of Sgort na Ciche (Pap of Glencoe) to the north, and the A82 road of traffic to Glencoe just over the river.

It was at this historic place that the two owls told the gnelfs to stay put and have a good rest, while they went in search of a meal of their own. The two eagle owls kind of hopped on one leg and then the other. Then they lifted up, and with a few whooshing flaps of their giant wings, they were gone, before either of the two gnelfs could say anything.

With the owls departed, Duncan and Isabella sat down to wait in the light drizzling rain, their clothing gradually becoming wetter and shinier as the time flicked on. Then as the sun rose higher, their clothing began to steam a little, which was a state of affairs Isabella was not too pleased about.

Duncan was the first to speak of the noticeable mess they were in. "What if the owls dunna come back?"

His little wife was looking through the lightly drifting misty *steam,* to far off into the sky above the hills, watching two specks in the clear heavens above that were the slowly disappearing pair of giant owls.

Isabella looked at her husband. "I dunna think that we will be bothered by the owl creatures this side of the next few days, Duncan!"

Duncan looked out in the distance. "Is that them over there, the wee specks in the sky?"

"Aye, that's them alright, an' they're goin' further away as we speak."

The two of them stood there for a few flicks of time before they realised that it was neither of them who had just spoken, the voice was too crusty.

Isabella looked at her little husband and asked a calm sort of question, in a calm but shivery sort of voice, "Who said that, Dunky?"

Her question was answered, but not by her husband, and in a gruff sort of voice, "It wer' me, your friendly badger…Mr Badger to you two, and it was me as did ken what the old owls wer' up to…They have done it before… They help folk along and then drop 'em to go look for food, and then, as soon as they find their food, they forget all about the new friends they have left waiting for them…You were, perhaps, too heavy for them anyway."

Isabella was annoyed. "So that's it, is it? That is how our new friends are going to treat us, eh, Dunky?"

Author's Note:
Gnelfs have a very keen sense of smell, which is not always an advantage.

Mr Badger shuffled a little closer to the two gnelfs, his big front claws digging and chuffing up the soft ground as he walked. His strong and strange smell got Duncan and Isabella before the badger got close to them, and before they could make any move to hide from it. The smell was awful, and one that neither of them had ever known before. It was as if they were being smothered by some sort of secret invisible cloud.

Duncan turned away as Isabella almost fainted with the shock of having to deal with such a nasty smelly aroma, and at the same time Mr Badger stopped to scratch himself; the huge front claw of his right foot spreading the aroma of his body smell by combing and scratching his fur away in big chunks.

After what seemed to be a lengthy smelly time to the two gnelfs, Mr Badger gave a long sigh and stopped his scratching to sit down in a curled position; the earth and grass somehow disguising his body smell just enough so as to make it possible for Duncan to approach him and ask a question, "How are we to find the island of Leodhais now?"

Mr Badger grunted for a couple of flicks of time, and then, he told the two gnelfs of a little secret he knew, "When I wer' a young badger, me mother said as I should go and travel around and find places where I might want to stay…And while I wer' travelling I came across a weird small chap in the hills not far from here, a little chap much like yourselves."

He looked at Duncan. "He had a white beard like you have, and he wore a green sort of coat and a kilt…But he was a lot older than you, I think…Yeh, he wer' a lot older…In fact, I don't know if he will still be there, now."

Isabella came closer, holding her nose by pressing her hand over it. "But if he *is* still there, could he help us? And what is a kilt?"

Mr Badger snuffled a wee bit. "I'm bobbity sure he could, yes I am…Proper bobbity sure am I." He looked at Isabella.

"A kilt is a skirt for a gentleman…or a lady."

"A skirt for a gentleman?" She looked at her husband Duncan. "You wearing a skirt! I've got to see that."

Duncan shrugged his shoulders. "I dunna think so." He then spoke to Mr Badger, doing his best to stay close to make sure Mr Badger would hear what he had to say, "Can you—"

Mr Badger butted in, "I know where he was last time I met him, but I'm not sure he will be there if we meet him again, *(think of that one slowly)* or where he is now."

Duncan was more understanding in the way of ignoring the smell of Mr Badger, and he could talk with him a wee bit easier than his little wife could, "We need you to take us to him if you will Mr Badger."

After spending a long time waiting for the smelly badger to finish his daytime sleep, the new trio walked slowly in the bracken and heather for what seemed ages and ages, looking for the nearest road of traffic to the north.

Mr Badger had said that it would be easier if they found the road of traffic and walked along by it to the north, but when they did eventually get to the road, it was beginning to go darker again; the dark night was coming, and they needed to find somewhere to sleep.

Isabella asked Mr Badger if he knew anywhere they could spend the night in the warmth. The old badger was surprised; he did not sleep at night himself. "Why do you want to sleep now? I am going to look for my food, and I will not be back until the new day begins."

He scuffed at his side with a back leg, the huge claws digging into his fur and disturbing more smelly aromas, their smelly horrible mixture mixing with the fresh air of the evening. "You should go and seek your food; it will be easy in the night dark."

Isabella told Mr Badger that she did not intend to wander off in the dark to look for food; she was more interested in finding a nice place to sleep. Mr Badger grunted a gruff reply.

"If that be what you wish, then I would suggest you both follow me."

Not long after following Mr Badger, the two gnelfs came to a fine-looking shady spot on a rise near a Silver Birch tree, the only tree of any great size for a good distance around.

Wishing the old badger a safe night dark, Duncan and Isabella settled down, sheltering under a large clump of bracken that grew right up to the silvery bark of the tree, where they curled up nice and warm.

The night dark was a quiet one when all things changed to morning light of day, and then the blowing breeze they had settled to, began to change, to a stronger gale of a wind.

"I don't like it, Dunky...I do not like it at all...It is too strong, and we are far from our new home...I don't like it," Isabella cuddled closer to her little husband as she spoke, her fingers fastening tight to the belt that went around his chubby waist.

Duncan was scared out of his wits really, but he could not let Izzy know that. "Oh, we will be fine Izzy...It will blow itself out soon, just you see."

Isabella buried her face in her husband's white beard and said nothing more as she gripped even tighter to his belt, wishing to herself that her little husband was right.

Duncan listened to the wind as it gained more strength, blowing the bracken around them as if it were a giant intent on seeking them out. He snuggled down with Isabella, wishing to himself that he was right, but knowing that, more than likely, he was wrong.

Some way off from the old birch tree, Mr Badger had paused for a moment to look back. But then, satisfied that the two little folks would have the sense to stay where they were. He snuffled a wee bit and then kept his black and white body low to the ground and out of the wind as he scrambled on.

When Mr Badger had gone, the gale force wind increased in power, and the birch tree began to creak and groan as it leaned over to take the strain, with the two little gnelfs becoming less sure of their safety with each creak or groan.

Putting his face close to the trunk of the old tree, Duncan asked it a question through its silvery bark, "Mr Silver Birch, can you be safe for us?"

The tree did try to answer, but it was too busy fighting for its own survival. The gale wind was pushing it fiercely.

Duncan spoke again, putting his face as close as he could to the tree so his words could be heard above the sound of the gale wind. "Mr Silver Birch! Can you? Or should we seek another shelter?"

The Silver Birch tree was brave to the end, but the gale wind was too strong for it, and its roots left the ground just as Duncan asked his last question.

The old tree leaned over with a groan, and then, bravely managed to say, "Go to the west and seek the old Gnome of Glencoe. Go, before the wind blows you away."

Duncan looked at his wife, and she smiled weakly and nodded. They knew they would have to go; there was nothing else for it. Like the old tree had said, if they remained they could be blown away to who knows where.

Little by little, the two gnelfs ventured out of their snug bed in the bracken and crawled along on their tummies, to rest behind a tuft of heather, the tops of which were being wafted this way and that by the gale wind.

It was a long hard and frightening night for the two brave gnelfs as they crawled along from one clump of heather to the next. But they eventually made it to the side of a stream of water, in a tree hollow where the gale wind could not reach, and the peace and quiet they found there was most welcome.

Isabella began to look carefully around for food; a few twigs and things, and just as the new light-day was opening, and the gale wind gone, the two of them were able to settle down to a welcome breakfast.

Duncan bit into a thick sort of twig and there was a cracking sound, he bit into the twig again and there was another cracking sound. He knew it wasn't the twig in his hand that was making the cracking noise, and he knew it wasn't Isabella. So, what was it? Had Mr Badger come back to them? On the other hand, was it someone else?

B'eòlach mo sheannar air
b-yawloch mo hennar ir
Well, my granddad knew it.

Chapter 6
The Old Gnome of Glencoe

More by luck than anything, Duncan and Isabella had made it to a small woodland area just to the east of the village of Glencoe.

Holding his breakfast twig halfway between his knee and his mouth, Duncan looked around, peering closely into the few trees that they had found shelter in by the clear running water. He knew something or someone was there, just behind the nearest tree to them.

"Come out now, I know you are there, come on out now!"

Isabella looked in the direction of the tree. "What is it, Dunky?"

Before Duncan could answer his little wife, an old gnome with a long white beard, and not much taller than Duncan, walked out from behind the tree and then began to float-walk towards them.

"Hello, my two friends, how are you? I am the Gnome of Glencoe…Who are you?" The gnome was polite and straight to the point.

Duncan thought it right not to delay in answering the old gnome, "I am Duncan Treggle, and this is my wife Isabella Treggle." He paused for a few flicks and then said, "We are gnelfs from the Isle of Arran."

Then there were a few moments of quiet before the old gnome continued.

"I am pleased to meet with Duncan and Isabella from the Isle of Arran…And where are you heading for?"

Isabella jumped in and told the old gnome that they were trying to get to the Isle of Leodhais.

"But why do you need to go there?"

The Gnome of Glencoe sat himself down by the two gnelfs and listened calmly and politely while they told him of their banishment from the Forest of Blackwaterfoot on the Isle of Arran, and that they had been told that they would find a good new home on Leodhais.

"Yes, there will be a good new home for you on the Isle of Leodhais, but first, you have many distances to go, and I know I can take you a little of the way. But the journey will not be easy, and there will still be many distances after that. I have to tell you that you are on a long, long journey my little friends, a long, long journey."

The Gnome of Glencoe kept his voice warm and kind to his new friends, and although he was right about the journey the two of them were on, the manner in which he spoke seemed to make it not so much of a problem, but more of the promise of a gentle voyage of discovery instead.

They finished their breakfast and the old gnome moved to take the lead, and, lifting himself up off the ground, he began to float-walk "You must trust me to take you the right way, it will be better for you."

He moved easily and slowly at first, allowing Duncan and Isabella to get used to the speed of his way of float-walking, their feet flicking the tops of the grasses and weeds as they moved along.

A few flicks of time later, and after a few bumps and scrapes, they came to a road of traffic busy with traffic; *traffic* every 10 flicks of time or so, and it was this *rush* of traffic on the road of traffic that upset Isabella. She stopped and grabbed hold of Duncan's arm. "We can't go this way; it is too risky for us, Dunky!"

The Gnome of Glencoe moved over to Isabella and talked to her quietly, calmly, and slowly, "You must not be concerned…I go this way all the time."

It was the way the old gnome talked that Isabella found so easy to hear, it made her feel safe just by listening to him. Even so, when he said that they were to find a ride on one of those traffic things, Isabella became a lot more than upset, and she would be even more so when she discovered the *traffic* she was going to ride on.

For a good many flicks of time, the three little folk made their float-walking way along the B863 road of traffic from Glencoe to Kinlochleven, where they came to a human picnic area in some trees, just off the roadway at the settlement of Caolasnacon.

The Gnome of Glencoe took the two gnelfs to a spot under the large wooden picnic table. "If you are able to keep the sun on your right in the morning and on your left in the afternoon, you will come to Oban in about a time-week, or two."

Isabella was baffled. "Weeks! I thought we would be there in a few light days…Not weeks!" She thought for a flick or two. "Just a flick, we've just come from Oban, haven't we Duncan?"

Author's Note:

A time-week to a gnelf is any number of days; it just depends on how far it is. I am sorry, but that is as near as I can get to how the gnelfs measure distance and time.

Duncan managed an *Err* when the old gnome spoke again, smiling as he talked when he told the two of them that it would take weeks, and when he saw Isabella so upset, he smiled even more.

"Oh, don't you be concerned so, if you like you can come to William's Fort with me, and then we can go by Loch Lochy to Invergarry together, and that way we will be quicker. And yes, you *have* been to Oban so you won't be going there."

Author's Note:

I am not sure what the old gnome meant, but I thought it best to just go along with it.

After agreeing to go to William's Fort and Invergarry, the journey became one of interest to the two gnelfs. They had never seen such lovely places as the ones they saw by the A82 road traffic, and they could not help but stop at different points along the way to admire the view and breathe in the clean Scottish air.

To begin with, although they did not know; the road that is, they began to float-walk along an old military road, (General Wade's Military Road) at the village of Torlundy, arriving there with the Gnome of Glencoe by float-walking along a railway line.

At the suggestion of the Gnome of Glencoe, the three little travellers stayed on the single platform of the Railway Station at Torlundy, and the gnome then said that they should catch a train to the next station at Spean Bridge.

After listening to Isabella going on about trains and how *not* to *catch* them, plus, the fact that she knew nothing about *trains*, the gnome assured her that travelling by train was easy; he had done it many times.

"I've even been to places many distances away on the train, no problem at all."

Author's Note:

It is true to say that Duncan and Isabella were fizz-icky at the prospect of catching *a train, but what would riding on a train be like?*

It was with some reluctance that Mr and Mrs Treggle agreed to catch the next train to Spean Bridge, and the three of them settled down on the end of the platform, hiding themselves in amongst the tall grasses that grew just by and through the platform fence.

An do dh'fhalbh an trean flathast?
na ghalav un trehn hah-ast?
Has the train left yet?

Chapter 7
Travelling by Train

They could not have known; not even by magic, that the next train to Spean Bridge would be pulled by a noisy steam engine, one that had started its journey from the town of Mallaig by the sea, about fifty distances away to the west.

At first, the far-off sound of the approaching steam-driven railway monster of an engine was a wee bit soothing in a way, and its steady distant regular chuffing and puffing seemed to create a sense of peace amongst the three little folk and their human soon-to-be fellow travellers.

Duncan even began to tap his foot to the rhythm of the chuff, chuff, and puff sound.

Then, things began to happen that were not so soothing.

Without Duncan and Isabella realising it, the chuff-chuff echo changed to the noisier sound of approaching smoking, steaming and hissing monster.

They looked in the direction of the noise, both of them alarmed as to what might it be approaching up the railway track towards them. Then they could see the smoking and chuffing monster coming ever closer as it came round the curve, then, as it got closer still, they could feel the wooden platform they were standing on beginning to shake a wee bit.

Whoof, chuff, whoof, chuf, whoof, chuf—

The noise was deafening, the trembling frightening, and Isabella hid herself in the flowers on the platform by lying flat on her tummy and pushing herself against the platform fence, while Duncan gritted his teeth and looked at the big steaming monster.

Taking great courage from being the Gnelf Elder, he spoke to the railway engine firmly, "Why do you make such noise? You could be nicer if you were a wee bit quieter."

Of course, although the old railway engine did understand, all it could do, in the way of answering the little chap, was to blow steam, covering Duncan in a shower of hot water droplets as it did so.

Shaking himself, Duncan spoke to the old railway engine again, but this time he stepped back to where the Gnome of Glencoe was standing, and near where Isabella was lying in the grass. "Would you take us to the next station, please, without a lot of noise?"

The old railway engine replied with a more satisfying whistling sound, and with the Gnome of Glencoe urging them on, the two gnelfs climbed on board with him and hid in an empty compartment of the carriage just behind the engine, *(a carriage door had been left open for late arrivals).*

With a slam, the carriage door was closed, and the old steam-driven monster chuffed very quietly to move forward nice and easy, with Duncan and Isabella hidden under a seat of the railway carriage that would be their home for the next 10 flicks or so.

Whoof, chuf, clickety-clack, whoof chuf, clickety-clack, whoof, chuf, clickety-clack—

The train rolled along at a smooth and steady pace, its rhythm making the two gnelfs relax a wee bit, and then, after about 10 flicks of travelling time, they peeked around and realised that they had the carriage to themselves. They went over to an empty seat, and, by helping each other up, they were soon sitting on the back of it, and able to look out of the window.

It was marvellous to Duncan and Isabella; with the landscape, which they had been part of not many flicks of time before, seemingly going by in a smooth movement they thought to be float-riding.

Author's Note:

The peace and calm of a gnelf can be seen in every buttercup and daisy, take a look one fine sunny day.

The trees and flowery bushes, and the view of the hills beyond, made Duncan feel a wee bit homesick, but before he could become too poorly, the Gnome of Glencoe interrupted their travelling by saying that they must be ready to get off the train quickly when they reached the station of Spean Bridge. Crawling along until the railway engine's brakes squeaked, bringing the train to a stop, with the front carriage stopping right at the end of the platform.

Duncan, Isabella, and the Gnome of Glencoe made their quick way to the door of the railway carriage in good time…But the door did not open, no human passenger was getting on or getting off.

Isabella looked at the gnome. "Why are we still on this train…train?" Duncan looked about him, trying to work out what to do. "I canna see how we can get off if the door dussnea (does not) open!"

The old gnome had gone back into the carriage, and he was under a seat and leaning calmly against the inside of the carriage. "Oh, it's alright, this sometimes happens... We'll just have to go on to the next station."

"And where will that be?" Isabella wanted to know the answer to her question before the train moved off, but she was too late, and as the train began to do its clickety-clacking again.

The gnome said, "Oh, that will be Roybridge where the River Roy meets with the River Spean." He thought for a few flicks of time. "And that is about four distances away."

Duncan breathed a sigh; he was happy that it was not too long a distance. "Oh, that's alright then, we will soon be there."

Author's Note:

What Duncan had not realised was that they were now travelling in the wrong direction altogether, and every clickety-clack *was taking them further away from where they wanted to be.*

The three travellers settled on the back of a seat again to watch the countryside go by, and Isabella asked a simple question that the three of them would learn a very important one, "And what do we do if the door dussna open at Roybridge, eh?"

Clickety-clack, clickety-clack, clickety-clack, and the train rocked slowly on, and within a few flicks of time, it rolled gently through the station at Roybridge without stopping.

Isabella was not amused. "Oh, that's truly silly, here we are on a train that is going to we don't know where, and we canna get off it."

The Gnome of Glencoe remained calm, not offended by Isabella's comment. "Oh, don't you go on so, it will be a nice ride we will be having. You stay nice and calm on the seat top and look out there, look how good the trees and hills are."

Clickety-clack, clickety-clack, clickety-clack, and the train rolled ever on, and without them understanding what it really meant to them, Duncan and Isabella began to enjoy the ride as they moved up Glen Spean; with hills and woods on either side, and passing by the hamlets of Achluachrach, Murlaggan, and Tulloch.

They were travelling through the Braes of Lochnaber and heading for the stopping platform at Tulloch Halt, which was a least two distances from Tulloch itself.

It was a smooth ride as the train took them through Tulloch Halt, *without stopping.*

With a look on her red face that said that as a newly introduced passenger to the railway, Isabella was not pleased, not one little bit, but she still spoke quietly and calmly, "Oh, I suppose we *will* stop sometime in the near future, eh?"

Neither the old gnome nor her husband bothered to answer the little lady gnelf, but instead, leaned over on the back of the seat as the train took a gentle curve to the right, heading for Loch Treig, and the heather and bracken-covered hills of the middle of the Scottish Western Highlands.

With the next station being at Corrour, and out in the wilds to the south of the loch, it meant that they still had a ride of about 12 distances ahead of them. Looking out of the carriage window at the calm water of Loch Treig, the three travellers were equally calm.

Author's Note:

Gnelfs, and gnomes, and elves, and fairies, never worry or become frightened; they just sometimes get a wee but niggly.

Isabella looked out at the big loch and spoke in a kindly sort of way, "It does look really nice doesn't it, eh? Lovely water and hills, with not a creature in sight, could it be that nothing lives out here because it is too wild? On the other hand, is it that most creatures can find their way to where they want to go without coming this way at all?"

Before she could continue, the train went into a tunnel and all went dark, and all that was said above the noise of the train's echoing clickety-clacking was, "Ooer," spoken by Duncan and Isabella together.

Within a few flicks of time, the train came back into the light of day with its whistle blowing, and Isabella looked out at the loch again. She was still looking when the train slowed for a little way as they came to a gathering of trees between the railway line and the loch. Then it stopped altogether, with the trees between the train and the loch directly by the door of the little folk's carriage.

The three small folk dropped down out of sight as the train's guard/ticket collector came to the carriage door and opened it, to jump down onto the trackside, leaving the door open.

The Gnome of Glencoe did not waste any time. "Come on, let's go." He made for the open door and then helped Duncan and Isabella go by him and climb down to the side of the track.

The two gnelfs clambered down and made it off the train, but before the gnome could make his own escape, the train guard/ticket collector came back; his booted feet crunching on the loose gravel, and the gnome had no choice but to rush back into the carriage, just as the carriage door was slammed shut.

Chuff-ruff, chuff-ruff, chuff-ruff.

The steam railway engine moved slowly and deliberately along the track, and away from where the two gnelfs were standing in the grass in the wooded area by the railway track. They were on their own again, and, after a few flicks of time spent in total disbelief, they made their sad way into the trees and looked around, and then they heard the cough of a stag.

Looking into the trees more carefully, Duncan was so surprised, and without doubt, so pleased to see Esknish the Stag, his head held high.

"Hello Esknish, how are you, it is—"

Duncan's attempt at talking with the giant stag was interrupted, with Esknish shouting back at the departing train as it chuffed and puffed its way out of their lives, "You will nae get the better of me, I only moved to let mysel' go to the water!" He gave another cough and then, spoke to Duncan, calmly, "Well, it is good to see you, little man." He looked at Isabella. "And you, Lovely little lady."

Duncan float-walked up to the big stag, his head only reaching just above the stag's hoof. "We are glad to see you Esknish; I was beginning to settle down to a long ride on the train monster when you stopped it…it was you, wasn't it?"

"Ach, nae bother…Where will you be going then, eh?" He did not wait for an answer and looked directly at Duncan and Isabella. "Are you two still making for the Isle of Leodhais over the sea then, eh?" He coughed lightly. "If that be the case, I'm afraid that you are a long way off the trail, in fact, you are going in the wrong direction altogether…You best come wi' me, eh?"

The stag walked, while the two gnelfs tumbled down to the edge of the Loch Treig, and sat or stood looking over the wide expanse of water at the steep hills on the other side.

Esknish spoke first, "I could swim it, but there is no way you two could swim to the other side, no way at all—" He then changed his way of speaking to a more high-born style. "Therefore, I would think it best we follow the railway tracks down to where there is a trail along by the bottom of the loch, and then, we must follow that trail until we come to the little Glen Leacach." \e paused for a few flicks of time and continued. "We then can possibly make our way up—" He stamped his right front foot. "Oh bother! Just follow me, will you?"

Although it was a long weary walk, floating or not.

Author's Note:

For a good part of the way, they and the Esknish could not float-fly, there was no mist.

The two gnelfs enjoyed the scenery, with the waters of the loch being with them all the way on their right and the view of the hills on the other side.

Esknish said nothing more and they carried on. Then they came to where the railway went away left, and to the east; that is where the big stag took them away from the railway track and began to make his way down a grassy path to the right.

With a thin mist just slightly around, the three of them walked, or float-walked, towards the bottom of the hills. They then turned to the right to start to make their way up the glen.

After going for about two distances, and after crossing three bridges, they came to the small patch of short grass, a soft green close-cropped natural carpet, and found it to be a good kind place to rest.

Isabella had enough, walking was not too bad if you liked it a lot, but she was not a real enthusiast. "That's it, I have had enough walking for one day. I am ready for some food and a nice long rest, and this looks like a good place to stay."

However, Esknish insisted that they should go a little further on. With his prompting, they made their way across the Cragan Lodge Bridge, over the stream of water that was the Aban River. They then found the little wood by the Ganach Hill and looked around at the lush grassland and the trees just up the slope to their left. Liking what they could see, they made their way up the slope to camp for the night.

The next morning, they found the hills shrouded in slowly lifting and drifting mist, ideal *flying* conditions for the big stag. "Come on, you two, we have a long way to go this day, and it is a good flying day." His voice growled in the still-enclosing blanket of a mist cloud and Duncan and Isabella reacted quickly, it's what gnelfs do.

With Isabella first to welcome the new light-day, she started to uncurl herself from the sleeping bed of grass. "Wha...What does he say, Dunky?"

Duncan Treggle gave an almighty yawn and tried to give a declaration. "This day I will—"

But he was interrupted by Esknish, "This day we will make many distances towards the island of Leodhais, so be awake and be ready."

There was no arguing with a giant of a stag, especially one who knew what was needed in the way of travel; he had done it many times before.

It was not many flicks of time later when the three of them were flying through the mist, with Esknish leading, his head held high with his nose sniffing out the way forward.

Duncan and Isabella followed the big stag closely, ever hopeful that he did, in fact, know the way, and ever hopeful they would get to where they wanted to be without misfortune. Even though it was thinning away, the mist stayed low in the glen and the three of them moved ever onward with ease.

As they flew through the mist, they floated over the little stream of Lairg, and then over two splashing waterfalls as they followed the rippling water to its starting place in the hills; about four distances from their overnight campsite at the Wood of Chunach.

Then the breeze freshened and the mist began to fade away, and the three odd travellers stopped their floating and began to walk by a hill. Keeping to the lower slope, they made their steady way along the path through the edge of the pine tree forest and then to Spean Bridge, further seven distances away.

As the gnelfs float-walked along, they kept the trees to their left and stayed on the path, and the big stag talked to his little friends about their journey, "You have a long way to go, my friends, and I am sorry, but I cannot go all the way with you; my lands only go as far as Spean Bridge."

They float-walked a little further and then the stag spoke again, "But I know of a hermit who lives in the woods by the little hamlet of Tirindrish near Spean

Bridge, and he will know of the way for you to go. You can trust him, he knows of the ways of gnomes and elves, and of the other creatures.

"He is an old Gaelic and he will talk with you in that language, but I know you will understand him, if you can talk with me, you are talk-wise with all humans and animals."

And so, it was. After bidding farewell to their good friend Esknish the Stag for the second time, Duncan and Isabella stood at the front gate of a tiny cottage in the trees above Tirindrish.

Just by the front gate to the cottage was a rowan tree of some great age, and it was this tree that shook its leaves and spoke to the two gnelfs as they stood pondering on what to do next.

"You have nothing to fear, the hermit is a good man, and he will make you feel at home in his cottage, just you knock on the door and wait."

Duncan thanked the tree, and then, he and Isabella walked up the short path to the cottage door.

S mah an sgàthan sùil caraid
sma hin ska-han sool karritch
A friend's eye is a good mirror.

Chapter 8
The Hermit of Tirindrish and the Treggles Become the Clan Mctreggle

"Should I knock on the door?" Duncan asked his little wife a question he should not have needed to ask.

"No, Dunky, just turn round three times and call out to the tree if it would be alright to stay in the garden shed for a wee while."

The little gnelf chap started to turn, and in a calm, he heard, "Duncan Treggle! Don't be so—" The gnelf lady demonstrated her verbal controlling influence of talking, and Duncan stopped turning, to knock on the door.

A few flicks of time later, a kilt-wearing and bearded old hermit came to the door. Without any problem or delay, the gnelfs were welcomed into the cottage; with a grace and kindness that made their lives that bit richer for knowing of such things.

It was soon clear to the old hermit that although they spoke in Gaelic, it was easy for the two gnelfs; they had known the old language from birth. And by speaking with him, it was as if they had at last found their true sense of birthright.

They were made to feel at home in a matter of a few moments, and treated to a meal of fresh green food from the forest, with a drink of a fine homemade herbal tea to round it off.

Authors Note:
A drop of herbal tea to a gnelf is more of just a whisper of a teardrop *on the end of a leaf to you and me.*

The hermit made Duncan and Isabella comfortable in his cottage home, and after they told him of their many long and weary distances of travel, he allowed them the luxury of staying with him for a few light days; helping them to regain their strength for the long journey that he told them was still ahead of them.

They talked at the end of each light-day about the different lives they had led, with the hermit telling his two new friends how he became a hermit in the first place.

The Hermit's Story. Translated from the Gaelic, with the help of Duncan McTreggle:

Some long time ago I met with an old man of the forest who was wearing an old kilt and a soft wool-like cap, with a folded blanket over his shoulder, and gripping a long wooden staff that seemed to be holding him up.

It was a cold rainy morning and I had just had my 12th birthday the day before, so I was a wee bit muggle-minded. The old man bid me to sit with him for a while and listen to his story.

I motioned at the rain, but he just shrugged his shoulders and loosened the folded blanket to allow it to fall over his knees as he sat on the trunk of a fallen tree.

I sat myself down with the rain pouring over me. But, and I still wonder at this, as he began to talk the rain ceased and the sun began to shine on the two of us in the forest, it was as if we were deserving of its true warmth, a consideration that was much like the warmth a body can often get after drinking a hot mug of sweet tea.

He gently told me of his first day in the forest, and how it came about. It was strange, but as he talked, I could somehow sense the passing of years, as if I was travelling through time with him.

His own story began with his memory of a battle fought bravely by many of his fellow compatriots, but it was a battle they lost. It would seem that he changed from that day, with him deciding to live alone in the wilds of the Scottish glens and hills, where he became content in remembering what had once been, but at the same time knowing in his heart that the old life had gone forever.

Author Note:

Duncan told me that as he and Isabella listened to the old man, he told his story in a whisper, with the lilt of the old Gaelic; his tone and pronunciation had been sharp but gentle to the ear, and he soon made two new friends.

The old hermit paused and looked at Duncan and asked if he knew of his Scottish family history, and Duncan had to reply that he knew nothing of his history, other than the fact that he had been born on the Isle of Arran and that he had lived there until he and Isabella had been made to leave.

He then looked at Isabella. "What of your family, my dear lady gnelf?"

Isabella liked the old hermit; he had a gentle way about him that made her feel safe and comfortable, even though he was a human. "My family is Duncan and me, and our children when they come along."

Isabella's honest reply made the old hermit chuckle. "If that is it, then, I know you will be happy together in your new home on Leodhais…First, we have a few things to sort out."

The old hermit then spoke to Duncan again, asking the little gnelf to join him in a room at the side of the cottage.

It was some flicks of time later when Duncan came back into the main room of the cottage. He looked magnificent in a kilt, with a threaded sporran, and a tunic of dark blue that fastened with a double row of sparkling brass buttons, and a pair of good woollen knee-high socks, and to top that he had a blue bonnet on his head.

Isabella was amazed; she had never thought her little husband could look so splendid. He was wearing a kilt of dark blue with crossing stripes of white, green and brown, *the tartan of the Clan McTreggles* as the old hermit put it. Although proud of his new style, when his dear little wife told him that he really did look to be a true gnelf, Duncan was even more proud.

The hermit spoke to Isabella nicely and politely, "Now, my dear Isabella McTreggle, what are we to do with you, eh?"

Isabella's answer was short and to the point.

"Not anything at all!"

The old and wise hermit did not argue, he knew better than that.

On the next light-day, after the three of them had eaten a good breakfast of leaves and twigs, the hermit picked up his long thin staff and made his way to the door of his cottage in a smooth gliding sort of walk. "Come on now, you two, we have a long way to go, and I am not in a hurry to hurry, but the sooner we start the slower we can go." *(Think about that for a minute, eh?)*

Even though what the hermit said was a wee bit out of the ordinary to the ears of the two gnelfs, they did see the sense of what he had said. If they started in good time, they could move along through the hills nice and easy; and as they later found out, when the mist came down the three of them could float in a gentle flight, a flight so gentle that there was not the slightest disturbance made to the free-floating mist around them.

Their first stopping place was in a small group of trees by the A82 road of traffic near Loch Lochy, and just under a bridge over a stream that flowed into the loch.

Being some 15 distances from Augustus's Fort, and although it was raining lightly, it did not matter to the two gnelfs. They were happy that they were on their way to Leodhais, and that their guide was the good Hermit of Tirindrish, a better guide that could not be found in all Scotland they thought.

They were right. Their guide was the best. He knew almost every nook and cranny of the Highlands and Islands, and as they walked and floated on, the gnelfs began to trust him more and more, even though they did not know how far they still had to go.

Authors Note:

To help you get your bearings, the three of them were in the Great Glen, and about eight distances south of Invergarry, with a further 10 distances north to Fort Augustus and the southern end of Loch Ness.

The rain continued, and Duncan and Isabella became a wee bit sad at such a dismal part of their journey. Nevertheless, the hermit was whistling softly as they made their way along through the rain, with his harmony making him happier the further they went.

Then, as the rain began to stop, and as if by some magic of signalling, they could hear the slight sound of bagpipes and drums way off in the distance, as if they were an accompaniment to the hermit's whistling, and a new brightness of sunlight gleamed around them.

The sound of the bagpipes and drums became clearer and louder as the marching band they were part of moved ever onward until Duncan and Isabella could not help themselves but start to jig and dance to the rhythm of the music being played.

Then it became distinct, they had come upon a group of pipe and drum bands playing the tune of a Reel *the Fairy Dance*, but it was a group of marching players with a difference.

At first, it seemed as though they were further away from the pipe bands than they had at first thought, the sound was sort of *quiet*, but when one of the bands drew near to where the two gnelfs were standing, it became clear to them that the pipers, and drummer, were little folk much like themselves. They were the Celtic Fairy Pipe Bands of The Great Glen, a truly well-kept secret that only the most Gaelic of Gaelic Scotland knew about.

Author's Note:

And now you, my dear reader, bless you.

One of the pipers came over to Duncan, and after allowing his pipes to sigh and lie to rest for a few flicks of time; and after politely greeting the three travellers, he asked the gnelf a question, "What is your tartan, my friend?"

Duncan could not speak at first, his mind was boggled with the piper's uniform and his pipes, but he swallowed and gave a good account of himself.

"Why, it is the tartan of the gnelfs of Steornabhagh, the Clan McTreggles, have you not heard of it?"

The piper looked at the hermit and smiled. He then began to prepare to play his pipes, with the instrument sighing and wheezing as he walked away to get back to his brother and sister pipers.

The Hermit of Tirindrish bent his knees and whispered to Duncan and Isabella.

"You will find that everyone you meet will know of the gnelfs of Steornabhagh, and the Clan McTreggle and their tartan, it is how we of the Gaelic share all good news—" He paused for a few flicks of time and then spoke about the rain. "We of the Gaelic can share good news like giving medicine to those in need, and even the rain can be good news on a dry day sometimes—"

He paused again and then spoke to Isabella, "I share the good news of sunny days with you, my dear lady gnelf, and long may you know of them through a long life."

Author's Note:

Now that was a really nice thing to say.

Càit a bheil sibh ag iarraidh a dhol?
kahtch uh vil shiv ug ee-urry uh gho<u>ll</u>?
Where do you wish to go?

Author's Note:

I have stood in the hills above Campbeltown and enjoyed a view of Scotland, a view of the stories of long ago. I can promise you that the story you are reading now does contain the spirit of old Scotland, and that of the old folk who knew it.

My sincere respects go to one who knew me and old Scotland, Terry Macfarlane, God bless his Gaelic memory.

Chapter 9
The Route to Augustus's Fort and Yet Another Ride on a Train

From the camp at the southern end of the little Glen Leachach to the town of Fort Augustus, was around 30 distances; with the first section being an early morning float-walk along the A82 road of traffic by Loch Lochy for the three travellers, to be followed by another float-walk along the same road of traffic by Loch Oich.

As they float-walked along, they talked in Gaelic, softly and kindly, as only Gaelic-speaking folk seem to do.

At first, Duncan had found it a wee bit odd talking to a human, but the Hermit of Tirindrish was very good at putting all creatures at their ease, and it was not long before he was talking calmly and nicely with the two gnelfs.

"Why is it you want to go to Leodhais, my little friends? Do you know what is there waiting for you? There are not many trees to speak of, and the wind comes off the sea in such a nasty mood sometimes that it's more than you can do to stand up."

Duncan tried his best to explain about their banishment from the Forest of Blackwaterfoot and the Isle of Arran, again, but the hermit could not understand why it was that living above ground was such a big problem.

"Why? I have lived above ground all my life and I haven't come to any harm, and I have met many good creatures like you two who do the same."

Author's Note:
There was a clue there for our two friends.

The hermit paused for a few flicks of time, and then, he began to explain something, "You need to get to a waterside place called Ullapool far north in the Highlands. When you get there, you must look for a cat by the name of Shipley.

64

She is the friend of a white witch who will get you onto the ferry to Steornabhagh without much trouble. So may all be easy for you, and I hope you enjoy your new home on Leodhais."

It was odd, but just a few flicks of time later, the two gnelfs were asleep, and the Hermit of Tirindrish sat down to work out and organise the remainder of their journey together along Loch Ness, to the little town of Invermoriston.

Then, making sure his two little friends were safe, he went to visit an old chum of his who loved right by the loch, and it was much later, when he returned carrying a cloth bag. He made a bed for himself, and within a few minutes, he fell asleep, his head resting on a smooth rock.

Author's Note:

There are many things that interest gnelfs of all ages, but the one thing *that interests them most is the wonderful work of Mother Nature. The little folk never tire of learning about the wonders of the natural world, and when Duncan and Isabella awoke the next morning, it was as if they had travelled in their sleep as if they had actually followed their dreams.*

Duncan had been dreaming of a sweet minnow-tickling spot by a loch, and Isabella had been dreaming of a nice new home in a forest of softly spreading and leafy branches.

As it was, when they opened their eyes fully, just in front of them, in the waters of Loch Ness, they could see fish swimming in a mass. They watched them gently waving their fins at them as they (the fish) swam this way and that right by the shore, and in a leisurely movement that seemed to need no effort at all.

Just to the right of where the gnelfs had been sleeping, there was a tree that leaned in a gentle kind of way over the waters of the loch; with its branches full of soft flickering leaves reflected in the shimmering water beneath.

The sight of the tree made Isabella sigh, and the sight of the fish made Duncan flick his fingers in preparation for doing some fish-tickling fishing.

The ripples on the loch fell gently on the bank as the sun in the sky shone brightly on the waters, but not dazzling so. A more special scene could not have been imagined, and for a long time, the two of them just sat and looked at the water and the tree in complete silence.

Then the Hermit of Tirindrish broke that silence, "We have to be going. This looks to be a good light-day for travelling, so it is best we do just that my little friends."

Accepting the persuasion of the hermit, Duncan and Isabella stirred themselves slowly, one tiny shrug at a time.

Isabella was the first to speak, "Where are we off to this fine light-day, Mr Hermit?"

Then Duncan added his questions, "How far is it? Are we having breakfast before we go?"

The hermit was kind. "Oh, 'tis only six distances to our first stop at Invermoriston, and then, we must take the high road through Glen Moriston for 16 distances to the Forest of Bunloinn. There we must rest for a while, for after that, we have a long way of 34 distances through Glen Shiel to the Eilean Donan Castle. There we will spend the night my little friends, and you will be welcome of the rest I can tell you."

Author's Note:

I am not sure why the hermit chose the route they took, but with him being the guide I think it is best we just let it be.

The journey started well, they had each eaten a good breakfast of leaves and such, and they were in good healthy form. Of course, with him being familiar with the path ahead, the hermit went in front; his kilt swishing as he walked and with his hand grabbing hold of his long walking staff he had fashioned many years before. The swing of the kilt and the staff helped him to keep up a steady walking and float-walking pace.

Duncan had quickly become used to his kilt, and this also swished as he and Isabella walked and float-walked, but only in a flickering sort of way, but where the hermit had a walking staff, Duncan had a dead twiggy dry branch off a hawthorn hedge.

It was some flicks of time after breakfast when they came to a group of hills called *The Five Sisters* by the side of Glen Shiel, and it was here at a human picnic spot by the A87 road of traffic that the hermit sat down and opened his cloth bag.

"Now then, my dear friends, it is time for you to learn one of the secrets of the Gaelic that will help you to find your new island home."

Duncan and Isabella were eager to see what was in the bag, but when the hermit took out an old ragtag piece of fusty smelly and dirty cloth, they were not so eager, and Isabella was not too pleased either.

"What are you on about, Mr Hermit? That is just a dirty bit of old cloth, is it not?"

The hermit responded calmly, "You are right, Isabella, but it is not just any old cloth, my dear. This cloth was once in a crofter's home on the Isle of Leodhais some hundreds of years ago."

Duncan made as if to take hold of the cloth, but the hermit pulled it away from him. "I must tell you the story of this cloth, and then, you will see why it is so important."

Author's Note:

The story of The Cloth *that follows, does have some connection to the truth, and it was only after I had written my version that I discovered this.*

Remember the truth, and follow the Cloth.

The Story of The Cloth
Translated from the Gaelic and as told by the Hermit of Tirindrish.

Some long years ago, the old Lairds of the Lands on the Isle of Leodhais made it sure and certain that all crofters, and other poor people, had to leave their homes.

On one drizzling and misty morning, a boy in a cottage near Steornabhagh picked up the cloth he and his family had known to be special. It was a hurried decision, as he and the rest of the family were being made to leave their home for the last time.

He took that piece of cloth with him all over the world, and when he was an old man in a far-off land, he gave the cloth to his grandson and asked him to return it to his old home on the island of Leodhais.

Now the son of that young grandson is an old man himself, and he lives in a cottage by the Loch of Ness, and he still had the little square of the cloth.'

All things have their value, but some are beyond price because of their value.

LH. H

Chapter 10
Isabella Meets the Cloth

The hermit held the cloth out to Isabella. "When you were asleep, I went to visit the old man, and he asked me to ask you if you could return the cloth for him. And he asked if you, the lady of our little party, he asked that you carry it with you and take it to the old home on the island."

Isabella took the cloth carefully, and when her fingers held it, she was pleasantly surprised to see and feel that it was really clean and soft to the touch.

She held it in her hands for a few flicks of time, and then, she held it up to her face. "It feels so soft, and I can feel the fresh breeze of the kindness of people who had known the Town of Steornabhagh and the island of Leodhais all those years long ago."

Author's Note:

I have felt the fresh breeze of kindness many times, and I hope you have too. However, if you have not, my wish is that you will very soon. Know it as you read the words in this story.

Isabella said no more, but the old hermit could see the look on her face that told him that the piece of cloth would be in safe hands. He knew it would be returned to its old home without fail. And as the little gnelf lady folded the cloth and put it in her belt, the old hermit could also sense the peace and love from a people long gone.

His old friend, who now lived by the Loch of Ness, would have been happy to see how Isabella had handled the bit of cloth and understood its real worth.

They carried on with their journey, and the two gnelfs were happy to follow the Hermit of Tirindrish in whatever direction he took, and along whatever trail he chose. Then, after two light days and dark nights, the three of them came to the hamlet of Achnasheen where the A890 road of traffic joins the A832 road of traffic in the middle of the Highlands.

To pause is to reach for the truth.

The Hermit of Tirindrish

Falbh thairisdhan taobh eile
falav harreesh gha<u>n</u> teav illuh
Cross over to the other side.

Chapter 11
The Cloth Shows the Way

The hamlet of Achnasheen was looking clean and fresh on a sunny and warm day, and the Hermit of Tirindrish said they should take the time to rest for a while, and decide what they should do next.

Then, with a sad but firm tone in his voice, he told the two little gnelfs that he could go no further; he had come a lot further than he had planned, and he had reached the end of his travelling and must return to his home in Tirindrish.

It was a bit of a surprise to the two gnelfs, they had come to rely on the old hermit's travelling skills a lot, and to know that he was going to leave them made them a wee bit uneasy, and a near tearful Isabella asked the one question she had not wanted to ask, "How do we find the way without you, Mr hermit?"

The hermit smiled at his little friends, and leaning over to Isabella, he said, "If you can't find the way, the Cloth in your belt will find it for you, don't you be concerned."

Isabella touched the Cloth in her belt and it was as if she *did* know the way, and her face lit up with the knowing of the way to go.

The hermit smiled again. "There, you see, it will be easy."

Duncan was not so sure. "How can a piece of an old cloth know the way to go?"

The old hermit put the little gnelf chap at ease. "I tell you, Duncan, it will be fine, just wait and see. While ever Isabella has the Cloth she will know the way to go, trust me; trust your little wife and the Cloth and you will be fine."

Then, after a quiet goodbye, the hermit walked off in the direction they had just come from. He was going to his home in Tirindrish, and the two gnelfs were now on their own again.

Still in need of finding the way to their home, they watched the old hermit until they could see him no more.

Then Duncan turned to his wife and asked a question of her politely, "Right then, Izzy, which way do we go then?"

Isabella looked down at the Cloth and then along the A832 road of traffic to the east and Inverness. "That's the way we go, Dunky, to Inverness."

She could not have said a weirder thing as far as Duncan was concerned. Going to Inverness was going the wrong way, he was sure of that.

"How can going to Inverness be the right way, Izzy? That's where the sun comes up in the morning. It's in my eyes when I wake up, it can't be right to go with the sun in my eyes when we should be going with the sun on me right shoulder!"

She paused to think. "But the Cloth is telling me to go that way, I know it is—" Isabella was calm, and certainly sure that she and the Cloth were right.

The sun climbed higher in the sky as they sat and waited for the Cloth to say or indicate a new direction, but it did not, not even when Isabella took it from her belt and laid it on the top of the warm stone wall. Then, as the Cloth lay on the wall, a chuff of a breeze blew one corner of it over another and made it point along the road of traffic to Inverness.

She was pleased at the Cloth's decision. "There you are, what did I tell you, now, it's definitely pointing the way."

Duncan could not argue, the Cloth was really pointing the way to go, and that way was going to be the way they would be going. After he had something to eat.

They walked, and they float-walked. If there had been some mist they would have flown, but it did seem as though the route to Inverness was a very long way to go. However, the Cloth did not falter, and the two gnelfs moved ever onwards. They had no choice. If they did not know the way; and they certainly did not, then they must go where the Cloth *says* they must go.

Then, just as they were passing by the little hamlet of Grudie, they heard the sound of a steam train someway off behind them; a sound they knew would mean that maybe they could ride to Inverness.

Grudie Station was about the same size as their last railway station, and within not many flicks of time, the two gnelfs were sitting calmly at the end of the platform, hiding themselves in amongst a pile of wood waiting to be loaded on the train when it arrived.

They were in luck, the train did stop, and the wood was loaded on the train on an open wagon, with the two gnelfs hidden nicely in amongst the wood.

As before, the 'clickety-clack, clickety-clack, clickety-clack' of the train was somehow soothing to the two gnelfs, and as they travelled on in comfort; their heads well below the woodpile, Duncan and Isabella began to feel sleepy, the smell of the wood not doing anything to keep them awake.

It was not long after leaving Grudie that the two of them were cosily fast asleep in the woodpile and travelling completely in the wrong direction yet again. Inverness would have been welcoming its first gnelfs if the Cloth had not done something about it. Something that to most of us would appear strange, but to the two gnelfs, it was something they were soon to be happy about.

As the train came near the next station at Garve, the Cloth lifted out off Isabella's belt by just enough to flap against her hand, the breeze from the movement of the train making it flap a wee bit more than usual.

"Wa…Wazzup? Duncan…we're on a train!" Isabella struggled up out of her *nest* in the woodpile. "We are on a train that is going in the wrong direction…look at the Cloth!"

Duncan lifted himself with the grace of a gnelf no longer interested in whatever direction they were going in. "So! Just lie down and get some sleep, we need—"

Isabella interrupted, "We need to get off this train, that's what we need to do, Dunky" She stood up and thumped her husband into getting up too. "Come on, Dunky, we have to get off!"

Creeping out of the woodpile, the two gnelfs made it to the edge of the railway wagon they and the wood were on.

Duncan looked down at the track going underneath them. "We can't get off here, the ground is moving too fast!"

He was right, it would have been too dangerous, to even *try* getting off. The only thing they could do was wait, but wait for how long though?

The Cloth came to the rescue again.

Right before their eyes, the Cloth changed colour, it went to red; the railway colour for danger and to stop. Even as the two gnelfs watched the colour change, the Cloth lifted up to the edge of the tall wagon behind their wagon. It flapped in the travelling breeze, lifted and attached itself to the edge of the tall wagon, to wave and flap madly on the outside of the wagon.

Some way off at the front of the train, where the engine was puffing and chuffing towards the station at Garve, the engine driver noticed the *flag,* some way back down the train.

The brakes squealed and the train gradually stopped, with the gnelf's wagon standing right by a bridge that carried the A835 road of traffic between Inverness and Ullapool.

Some flicks of time later, after the driver had done his checks, the train had gone, its chuffing and puffing sound someway off along the railway track to Inverness, and Dunky and Izzy were moving off the bridge; the Cloth wafting and waving in the direction they needed to go, along the A835 road of traffic to the north.

The two gnelfs did know it, but they were further away from the island of Leodhais than they were the light-day before, and they were more than 60 distances from the ferry town of Ullapool. From there, they would need to make a sea journey to their new island home, their last *over the waters* voyage.

The weather was kind, with a slight breeze blowing from behind them, and making their float-walking a wee bit faster than normal.

They float-walked along easily and carefully, but their legs and arms were aching a wee bit from their climb off the railway wagon and up the bank to the bridge.

Isabella made a *state of a warning* to whoever might care to listen, "Travelling on the railways is not nice if you are little, and when your Cloth can keep telling you not to, it is best not to."

Duncan held out his arms and let the wind lift him slightly as he floated along with his feet, not more than two *tickles* off the tarmac at the very edge of the A835 road of traffic. Isabella took a deep breath and followed her husband at the same sort of *reckless speed*.

Of course, it was only a matter of time before one of them came to a stop, a short sharp stop, and that was Duncan.

He had noticed how there seemed to be many streams of water coming down off the hills on his right. And as he tried to take a closer look at one near a hotel, he stumbled on the grass at the side of the tarmac road of traffic.

His head did its best to get wherever he was going before his feet could get there and his tumbling continued. Then, after tumbling this way and that for a few times, he found himself at the bank of the little River of Inchbae, some five metres down the bank from the road of traffic and a hotel.

Isabella did not panic; gnelfs do not do that anyway. She made her way down the banking carefully, holding on wherever she could, and sliding a wee bit where she could not.

They could hear the traffic on the road of traffic for a little while, and then it would stop and all would be quiet. Then it would start again, with a few traffic things speeding by.

All the time that the traffic did or did not go by, Duncan rested where he was; his feet in the water with the rest of him lying down on the soft and warm grassy bank.

Isabella sat by her husband but did not put her feet in the water, she was a gnelf lady, and lady gnelfs don't do such things.

Then, as light-day began to change to night dark, the traffic on the road of traffic stopped altogether, and the night dark began to crawl up the glen. A night dark would mean they would be on their own in a part of the Highlands they had never been in before and did not know anything of it and its history.

Author's Note:

Gnelfs have a real interest in the history of lands and things, they call history-story, *and for a gnelf to be somewhere they did not know the story of was a case of mystery, and sometimes a real bother for them. Now, to Duncan lying and Isabella sitting by the little River of Inchbea, it was more bothersome than just a mystery.*

As the night dark got even darker, the lack of a history-story got more and more bothersome.

Isabella said what she thought should be said, "I can't be doing with this...We do not know where we are, or of the history-story of the place; where we do not know where we are...and I am tired."

Duncan stretched his arms above his head and took his feet out of the cold water of the river. "Yes, my dear, I am tired too. So, let us—"

Isabella interrupted, "I am not yours, or anybody's *deer*, I am a gnelf lady—"

Even as Isabella had said what she had said, she had the thought that she was more tired than she had at first realised. And before Duncan could say that he did not mean *deer* but *dear*, she dropped her head, sank back on the grassy bank of the river, closed her eyes, and fell asleep.

The gnelf chap with the wet feet made no effort to argue about the *deer* versus *dear* business. His little wife was asleep anyway. He just let himself sink into the grass and allowed his wet feet to stick up in the air a wee bit.

74

Feet could dry in the night dark if he let them waft about in the wind, and he need not bother about them. With this thought on his mind, Duncan McTreggle pulled his kilt between his knees, and let his head softly drop into the pillow of grass that Mother Nature had thoughtfully provided for such an occasion. And within three or four flicks of time, he was asleep by the river, and snoring politely so as not to wake Isabella.

Dè cho tric 's a chì thu e?
jae choe treechk suh chee oo ch?
How often do you see him?

Chapter 12
Marlow Mulzie and the Road of Traffic to Ullapool

Of course, everyone knows that there are all kinds of creatures that live in forests, creatures that are sometimes seen, and some that are not. However, in the forest where Duncan and Isabella had slept by the river, there was one creature person who had never been seen by anyone; but one that had always made it his business to see all others who cared to visit his forest and river.

Giant rabbit Marlow Mulzie was the slow/fast-moving creature of the Forest of Corrie who had been watching the two gnelfs with interest, right from the moment they had arrived at the riverside.

He had been making his way by the hotel, looking for interesting human people to watch when he had come across Duncan and Isabella by the river. They had seemed to be of more interest than a mere human or two, in fact, he was sure he had never seen the like before.

Marlow was a rabbit, a rather big rabbit with big, long ears, and he was a rabbit who did not care for *bobbitting about* as his cousins in the fields seemed to like doing. No, he would rather just sit up in secret and look about him and try and find interesting things and creatures, and humans, to just sit and watch them.

He had found that they all do different interesting things if he watched them for long enough. The humans were the best, they made him smile a lot, and they were so silly at times.

But these two little creatures he had been watching on that night dark were different, he could sense it somehow, and even while they slept, he could feel a certain liking for them. It was as if they would know him, which was a strange thought, but one he could not get out of his fuzzy head.

Delicately balanced we move on…ready?

Isabella opened her eyes and sat up, and as her eyes woke up with her she looked across the water and spotted the biggest rabbit she had ever seen.

"Duncan! Duncan! Wake up, Duncan…There's a rabbit!"

Duncan rolled over and looked across the top of the grass at the water where his feet had dropped back into the river while he had been asleep.

"Oh…a rabbit…How nice for you—"

He rolled back and closed his eyes, to enjoy the feel of the river water caressing his feet in a cold embrace, a feeling he could not be bothered to bring to an end.

Isabella reached over and shook her husband. "No, Duncan, not a rabbit…A BIG RABBIT!"

The damp ruffled around the sleepy Duncan's feet, tickling between his toes in a cool but loving fashion.

He spoke without opening his eyes, "Yes, my dear, a rabbit is a rabbit, and you have seen one…nice for you, my dear."

Ever and ever on…still ready?

The foot that kicked him was covered by a soft shoe, but the kick was a lot harder than the shoe.

"Duncan McTreggle, open your eyes and look across the water. Come on, get up and come look!"

The wet feet left the grass, and Duncan McTreggle got up, or let us say that he sat up on one elbow.

Duncan opened his eyes very slowly and looked across the little River Inchbae.

"Why didn't you wake me earlier? That's not a rabbit, it's a *rabbit-rabbit*!"

Across the river, Marlow licked his paw and wiped his face, and then, he pulled one of his huge ears down to his mouth so he could lick that too.

Then, with his morning wash over, he called to the two on the other side of the water, "Good early day-morning to you, my friends…I am Marlow Mulzie, the Rabbit of Strath and of this glen, and of many other glens as far as the eyes can see…Who might you be?"

Still, we move ever onward.

The big rabbit twisted one of its ears forward a wee bit to catch the sound if either of the two were to understand what he had said and would speak back to him. He did not know for sure that the little folk had understood what he had said, but he was soon to learn that gnelfs do understand all language, even rabbit talk.

Duncan stood up, and ignoring his wet feet, he shouted across the water in rabbit talk.

"Good light-day, Mr Marlow Mulzie. I am Duncan McTreggle and this is my dear wife Isabella McTreggle."

Isabella whispered to her wet-footed husband, "I am not a *deer*, Duncan!"

Marlow's big ears never missed a thing, especially in rabbit talk, and he told Isabella that he knew she was not a *deer*.

The river water trickled by for a few flicks of time while the two on one bank and the one on the other looked across at each other. Then, Marlow walked back a few steps and then leapt into the air.

Yes, ever onward.

Duncan and Isabella had seen rabbits jump before, but Marlow Mulzie was a *rabbit- rabbit*, and when he jumped, he made it look as if he was flying.

In a matter of a few slow and easy sniffs of his big nose, and a few tiptoe touches on the river water with his big feet, he was standing by the side of Isabella.

The sniffing and twitching nose of the sitting-up rabbit was high above Isabella's head; higher than she could reach, and she decided that the rabbit's big feet at the side of her were the biggest and widest furry feet she had ever seen.

Duncan could not work it out, how could it be that a rabbit could be so big?

"How is it you are so big? The rabbits we have met on our journey so far have all been soft and fluffy, and a lot smaller than you."

Marlow spread his big front feet and dropped his head down so he could speak nicely to his two new friends. "I will let you into a little secret, a secret that other rabbits don't know—"

Author's Note:

The story of Marlow Mulzie, translated from the Gaelic, and as told by Marlow himself. Talking to little folk is one thing, but talking to a giant of a rabbit who grins all the time, even through a translator; well, my dear reader, that was something else entirely, but I noted down what he told us.

Also of note is the fact that, as much as I would wish to, I do not speak the beautiful Gaelic language, and my translator Duncan McTreggle is more the author of what follows about Marlow than your writer.

Marlow Mulzie's story:

When I was a little baby rabbit, my mum told me I should eat plenty of oats, to make me big and strong, and because of that I have always been a big rabbit, a fast-running big rabbit.

I lived in the fields for a long time, but it seemed that I was always getting in the way of the other rabbits and that they were always getting in my way. When it came to hiding in the underground dens, the burrows as they call them, I could not go down them because I was too big. And I stopped digging my own burrow dens because it was too much hard work just for one rabbit.

The other rabbits started to complain that I was too big to be in their fields, and when I moved, the rabbits I moved to be with, said the same after a while, and I had to move again.

I began to realise that I had no choice, and in the end, I had to accept that I would have to find a home for just me and a home above ground.

After roaming about for a long time, sleeping here and there in hiding places that were okay for one sleep-time, I made the choice to live in this Forest of Strath and wander around in the summer in other woodlands of the Highlands.

I have met with many different folks in my time in Strath and the rest of the Highlands, and I have gotten to know some kind and interesting creatures and humans.

—Ready—

Duncan liked the old Rabbit of Strath, he was so soft and fluffy, big and kind, and he had nice big floppy ears. "Do you like living above ground Marlow? Is it alright and—"

He paused to think, but Isabella jumped in without giving Marlow the chance to answer, or for Duncan to ask more silly questions, "Can you...Do you know of a place called Steornabhagh? On the—"

She paused, and it was Marlow's turn to interrupt, "Oh yes, that's a town by the sea on the Isle of Leodhais, I went there once when I was little...I had to tiptoe onto a ferryboat in the night dark. I was really small then, so it was easy."

Duncan and Isabella spoke together, "You have been there?"

But it was Isabella who continued, "Do you know where the ferryboat is?"

The big rabbit sighed and licked the end of one of his big floppy ears again, holding it to his mouth with a big front paw.

Then, licking over, he answered the gnelf lady, "Oh yes, of course, I do. I go near there often…But I don't go on the ferryboat anymore, the ferry folk would catch me. I'm too big to hide now, you see."

Duncan was really sitting up now. "Could you show us the way, Marlow? It would be really kind of you if you could, you see—"

He looked at Isabella and she nodded to him and continued the conversation by saying what her little husband was about to say, "You see, Marlow, we had the same problem as you…We once lived on the faraway Isle of Arran, but because we wanted to live above ground they made us leave, and we were told to go find Steornabhagh and make a new home for ourselves above ground there—

"We have travelled a long way to get here, and we would really love to get to our new home soon, it would be so nice to make a home."

Marlow shuffled his feet and twitched his big whiskers, and then said that he would be more than happy to show them the way. In fact, he said that he would go with them as far as the little pretty town of Ullapool; from where the ferry to Steornabhagh sailed.

Isabella was happy for herself and Duncan; happy and fully relaxed. Somehow, she knew they were getting close to their new home now, and that Marlow Mulzie, the Rabbit of Strath, would be their new guide to the ferry.

Of course, she was right, they were getting close, but what she did not know was that, they still had 30 distances through the Highlands to go and that there would then be a journey over the big sea waters to their new island home.

Marlow was amazed at the gnelf's ability to float-walk, and he asked them to show him how to do it, with his mind set on learning to float-walk before they set off on the journey to the ferry port at Ullapool.

Author's Note:

Be there if you can.

Author's Note:

When Duncan told me about Marlow's first attempts at float-walking, it made me smile. But I would think it better if I could be kind, and just tell you that

Duncan said the big rabbit bumped around for a bit, but then he did, in fact, learn how to float-walk in the best tradition of the float-walking gnelfs.

If ever you see a big rabbit moving very fast, it might be that it is float-walking Marlow Mulzie or one of his floating *cousins. You never know.*

The three friends made their steady way along the A835 road traffic, passing by Loch Glascarnoch without having any trouble with traffic. If they heard a traffic coming they just sat down in the long grass by the road, with Marlow hiding behind a bush or tree, until the traffic had gone.

Although they did hear the rushing waters of the Falls of Measach, the two gnelfs did not see them, content instead to carry on, with Marlow telling them that they were getting really close to Ullapool.

"We can rest at Inverbroom for a wee while, and then, we have only to go by Loch Broom for about six distances and we will be there."

The two gnelfs had come a long way since the Elders of Blackwaterfoot Forest had banished them from the Isle of Arran and caused them to be immigrants. Now, they could almost smell and hear the big seawaters, the long journey through the Highlands was gradually becoming a memory they would never forget, and one they would later remember with some affection, especially when thinking of the creatures and folk they had met on the way.

Just up the road of traffic from Ullapool, in the small, wooded Glen of Achall, Marlow said that he could go no further; the folk in the town would see him and would think him to be strange, and he would not like folk to think of him in that way.

Duncan thanked the big rabbit for his kindness in bringing them to the place of the ferry and asked if he could advise them on how they could get to and on the ferry.

The big rabbit fairly brimmed with pride, and smiled with the pleasure at the chance to tell them about someone who he knew would be more than happy to help them. "But first you have to wait around here until Shipley the Cat finds you."

Isabella had not met a cat before, but she had heard tales of how they can be a wee bit hissy-fissy and changeable. "Will Shipley the Cat be kind to us? It is not going to—"

Marlow was smiling. "Oh, you have no need to be concerned about Shipley. She is the kindest cat this side of the Highlands, if not in all Scotland."

Marlow was almost purring like a cat himself as he talked with the two gnelfs, telling them of how it was that Shipley had made it right for him to go on the ferry sometime before.

"But it is not Shipley who will take you on the ferry, my little friends, no. It is that she will take you to see the White Witch of Ullapool first, and if you can be a friend to the witch, it is she, who will take you on the ferry to Steornabhagh."

Marlow then went on to tell of how the white witch will not meet with any creature or folk who have not been brought to her by Shipley. "It is the way she likes it, but I can tell you, if the white witch takes a liking to you she will make sure you get where you want to go safely."

He licked his paw and then wiped his face, and then, said goodbye to the two gnelfs, "I will be off now, my little friends, just you wait about here, and before long Shipley will find you."

Duncan and Isabella watched the big rabbit float-walk away back up the road of traffic they had just come along together, and where the road of traffic went round a bend Marlow turned and waved a last farewell. Then, he was gone, and the two gnelfs were on their own again, in a strange land by the big sea waters.

Cha dèan e cron ort idir
cha jee-an eh cron orsht eejir
It won't harm you.

Chapter 13
Shipley the Cat, and the White Witch of Ullapool

Duncan and Isabella had left the Isle of Arran to get to the mainland, and now, they were seeking a way to leave the mainland to get to the Isle of Leodhais, their new island home out in the Western Sea.

First, Shipley the Cat must find them before anyway, or effort could be found to get them to their new island, and it would seem that there was no way the two gnelfs could do anything to make this happen.

"How do you get a cat to find you?" Duncan asked the question to himself really, but Isabella thought it best to answer him; he would ask her later anyway.

"I would say that a cat will find what it wants to find, and when it wants to find it. So, I would say you don't get a cat to do anything about finding us, the cat will do it in its own good time."

On a tiny plot of land near Ullapool, and right by the shore of Loch Broom, there is a small white-painted cottage. The two gnelfs could see it from their sitting place by the road of traffic leading down to Ullapool; they were about one distance from the town.

They could also see that as the sunlight gleamed over the loch and the cottage, the scene took on a dreamlike quality that painter-artists love, cottages that seemed to share with the land and the water in a nice sort of way.

Isabella looked at the distant cottage and sighed. "Now, look at that, Dunky, isn't it lovely? A white cottage by the still waters of the loch. Wouldn't you like to—"

She stopped talking as she spotted a black and white cat walking up the road of traffic towards them, its tail erect and slightly fluffy.

The fluffy cat came to the gnelfs and said nothing; it just sniffed around them, and then, sat down in front of them, and waited, as if it was waiting for one of the gnelfs to speak. Not true, however.

When Isabella made it as if to speak, the cat hissed in a low voice, "Shh…shush. I will speak now. My name is Shipley, and I live in the white cottage by the loch with my Mistress Merrill, the White Witch of Ullapool."

The cat looked at the two gnelfs carefully, its whiskers twitching and with a kind of secret smile on its face.

Duncan spoke in a whisper, "Good day to you, Miss Shipley…Could we? Would it be possible for us to meet with your Mistress Merrill? We would…We have been told that you can help us to get to the island of Leodhais out in the Western Sea."

Shipley began to purr, with her smile widening. "It was my Mistress Merrill who told me to come and find you; she knew you would be on the way to us you see." The cat talked so smoothly, that it made Isabella shudder with a kind of gentle pride, and she was surprised.

"But how would she know we—"

The cat purred louder and then spoke and interrupted the gnelf lady, "You should not ask such questions; you will soon learn that Mistress Merrill has special powers. Powers we should not ask about but just accept."

The two gnelfs looked at each other, and Duncan said something he did not know he could say, "Magic is magic when magic is known to be magic."

Shipley smiled even more as she listened to the gnelf. She had met many creatures on the road of traffic down into Ullapool, but she had never met such kind as the two gnelfs. Little folk, she knew would be kind and thoughtful to all they meet, she could tell it was in their nature, and she knew that her mistress would be happy to see them.

Mistress Merrill was waiting for them as they walked along a path by the loch; a path that went from Ullapool to the white witch's cottage, which, like most of the cottages of Ullapool, was a whitewashed low-roofed building of old age.

Pause and rest for a wee while.

Author's Note:

Before we carry on with the story, it is best that I explain that Mistress Merrill and Shipley could understand each other, and the gnelfs, with all of them speaking in Gaelic, or in the case of Shipley, in a cat version of the Gaelic.

Shipley the Cat introduced the two gnelfs and then, sat down in some short grass by the path while Mistress Merrill spoke with the two little folks, "Hello, my little friends, from the Isle of Arran. I am so pleased to meet you…Will you join me by the loch? I have made us a cake for the occasion, and I have chairs and a table by the waters that will help us to enjoy the cake and the loch at the same time…Come with me, my friends, let us be good to the loch."

There followed a quiet time, and then Mistress Merrill began to turn; her earrings and bangles turning with her, but as she did so she spotted the Cloth in Isabella's belt, and then the witch's face began to change to a more blushing tint.

She knew what the Cloth was, she knew in her heart what it was, and her whole body shook with excitement of knowing what it was. Her breathing was quicker, and in a weird sort of way, it was as if her eyes were glowing.

She spoke to Isabella, her voice trembling slightly as she was unable to hide her excitement, "Where did you get the Cloth, my dear?"

Isabella started to say that she was not a *deer*, but a nudge from Duncan stopped her. She politely said that the Cloth had been given to her by the Hermit of Tirindrish, with the instruction to take it back home to Leodhais.

Mistress Merrill was sighing with gratitude, and then she explained to Duncan and Isabella that it was the most exciting thing that had ever happened in her long life.

"You are blessed with the task of returning the Fairy Flag of Leodhais to its home, it has been missing for hundreds of years, and *you* are taking it home; you have been blessed, my Dears."

Isabella could see that there were tears in the white witch's eyes, and she went over to the lady, and tugging at the hem of the witch's skirt, smiled a smile of comfort to her. "I promise you, I will take care of it, Mistress Merrill. Duncan and I will make sure it finds its home again. We will—"

With her voice full of joyfulness, Merrill interrupted, "Oh, my dear little lady gnelf, I could not see you having to take it on your own! I will be very happy indeed to take the two of you, and the Fairy Flag of Leodhais, to your new home in Steornabhagh on the lovely island of Leodhais. It will be one of my most proudest moments, to be there to take the…It will be my most pleasant duty."

After a few more sighs and steadying of breath, Mistress Merrill calmed down, and they all went down to the shore of the loch to *take tea* in the warm sunshine of a misty Scottish summer evening.

The last part of the gnelf's long journey was now in sight, and Duncan and Isabella knew they would soon be home. It was a good feeling.

As the four of them sat by the loch, with Duncan and Isabella sitting at the low table on highchairs, it was Isabella's turn to give a long sigh, a sigh that was not missed by Merrill.

"Don't you worry, my dear, your journey will soon be over, and you and Duncan will be in your new home, I will make sure of that, I promise you."

Isabella relaxed and looked out over the loch, watching with interest a seagull swooping and swerving over the waters they would soon be crossing on a boat; the CalMac ferryboat that she somehow knew would have to be a big one.

Chapter 14
The Ferryboat to Steornabhagh, and Taking Home the Fairy Flag of Leodhais

The white-walled Scottish port of Ullapool was busy, and the Motor Vessel Isle of Lewis, the CalMac ferry to Steornabhagh, was waiting at the port landing stage.

People and cars were going on board the big black and white *CalMac*. Amongst them was a smartly dressed lady with a bicycle; a bicycle with a basket with a lid on the front, and a large basket with a lid on the back.

In the basket on the front, Duncan and Isabella McTreggle were laid back comfortably on a soft cushion. In the basket on the back, Shipley the cat was curled up on her favourite mat. They were set for the Isle of Leodhais, and a new life for the gnelfs in the front basket.

Mistress Merrill wheeled her bicycle onto the ferry and made her way to be near the front, to sit on the seats provided for passengers to enjoy the view of the waters, waters she and others knew of as *the Minch*, but which her new friends the gnelfs thought to be the *Big Sea of the West*.

The warning horn of the ferry told all who cared to take notice that it was about to set sail for the far-off western Isle of Leodhais, and from deep within the boat the engines could be heard rumbling and mumbling with their power.

In the basket on the front of Mistress Merrill's bicycle, Duncan stiffened in emotion, he had never heard such a sound before.

Isabella on the other hand spoke kindly about the motor sound, "Isn't that a lovely sound, Dunky? It is like music to me."

Duncan relaxed a wee bit and said that he would prefer it if the ferryboats were not so eager to make noises like that.

At the same time, in the basket on the back of Mistress Merrill's bicycle, Shipley the Cat curled that bit tighter and went to sleep; she knew it would take about two and three-quarter hours to get to Steornabhagh, and she had seen all there is to see for a cat on a ferry.

Mistress Merrill sat looking out at the land as it seemed to slip by as the ferry gained a little more speed to take them across the Loch of Broom and out onto the *Minch Sea.*

This was the part of the journey she liked the most, the beginning. Floating out to the big waters and towards the old world of Leodhais, the old world she loved and could never visit enough, and with every visit being like going home and beginning again. Maybe, one day, she will.

Mistress Merrill's story and the story of the Fairy Flag of Leodhais.
Translated from the Gaelic, and as told to me by a lady of Steornabhagh who became my good friend:

It was back in the days when hurrying was not so much a problem. There was no need to hurry at all. Mistress Merrill at the age of 10 was quite happy to help her mother with all kinds of chores, such as feeding the chickens in the morning and evening. But she always seemed to have time to read and to take time to be kind.

It was a good life in the village of Pabail on the neck of land called Eye, *about 10 distances from Steornabhagh. As she grew up and became a young woman, she learned of a secret that many of the old islanders had known for a long time.*

It was the secret of the Fairy Flag of Leodhais, a Cloth she thought she and the others would never see; having been told that it had been taken from the island many years before, and to who knows where, and maybe lost forever to the folk of Steornabhagh and the Leodhais islanders.

The Fairy Flag of Leodhais had been given to a clan chief at the time of a battle in the years of long ago, with the promise that the flag would save all who cherished it from danger, and in times of need, it would show the way forward.

The Clan Chief's cottage home had been the safe resting place for the flag for many years, but when the island had been cleared by the lairds and landowners, the flag had been lost.

It was with some kind of fairy interest that Mistress Merrill became a witch. Even at an early age, she had known the fairies that lived on Leodhais, and she had been on her own one day when one of them spoke to her, not in a loud voice but in a soft restful kind of way, telling her that she was of magic and of good.

As the years went by, Merrill understood more of the magic, and she became more at ease with her life as a witch. As she grew older and more familiar with the witching ways, her fame spread all over the Western Isles and the west coast of Scotland.

Many folk in Steornabhagh, and the rest of the island of Leodhais, began to ask her for magic help she was too happy to give, and in this way, she became a kind and generous white witch.

On her 50th birthday, she took the ferry to Ullapool and moved to a new home near that lovely town; in the white cottage by the loch where she still lives to this day.

...

It was a good few more flicks of time later when Duncan woke up again to listen to the strangely comforting sounds of the ferryboat, the mumbling bumbling of the engine below the deck, the chatter of human folk, and the whisper of the wind blowing off the sea.

As their journey on the ferryboat continued, the little gnelfs had started to become fond of the noises. When Isabella woke up a few flicks of time further on and said how she liked the sounds of the ferryboat taking them to their new home, Duncan had to agree.

The ferryboat MV Isle of Lewis made a smooth and calm landing in the harbour at Steornabhagh; Merrill took hold of the handlebars of her bicycle and made her slow and easy way off the ferry, and into the town of Steornabhagh and onto the island of Leodhais, her old homeland and now the gnelf's new home.

The young folk on the harbourside paid little attention to the old woman with a bicycle, but some of the older folk of the town needed only to look once to know who she was, and Merrill was soon exchanging greetings with them. They wanted to speak to her, to say hello, and in one or two cases, to ask if she would care to share a meal with them, offers she politely declined.

Mistress Merrill said nothing about her little friends in the front basket of her bicycle, but she did lift Shipley the Cat from her resting place in the basket at the back of her bicycle, and introduce her to everybody, and Shipley purred and strutted along by Merrill's feet, pleased and happy to be back on the Isle of Leodhais again.

Putting Shipley the cat back in her basket, Mistress Merrill waved goodbye to the old folk who had walked along with her for a while. She then climbed on her bicycle and began to pedal towards her home village of Pabail, taking the A866 road of traffic by the little airport.

...a different kind of moving on...

As soon as they had left the town of Steornabhagh behind them, Mistress Merrill lifted the flap on the front basket of her bicycle and allowed Duncan and Isabella to see their new island for the first time.

Isabella lifted herself as high as she could to look over the rim of the basket. As she did so, The Cloth that was now The Flag in the basket with her, flew off and landed by the roadside, with one corner of it flapping and waving gently as it lay on the ground.

Mistress Merrill calmly put her bicycle on its stand and crouched down to talk to The Flag, "We have brought you to your homeland, and we will be happy to take you to your old home if you can show us the way."

The Flag rippled along the ground for a few flicks of time, and then as if having found the way, it lifted off the ground and fluttered off along the road of traffic towards Mistress Merrill's home village, but after just a few bits of distance, it flung itself down a grassy track to the right, in the direction of the Village of Cnoc.

Mistress Merrill told Duncan and Isabella to sit back down in the front basket, she then closed the lids of the baskets and then mounted her bicycle and followed The Flag as it waved and weaved down the grass-covered track.

After something like 10 flicks of time, (twenty minutes or so perhaps) The Flag swung gracefully to the right and stopped by the wall of the garden of an old cottage, an old crofter's cottage. It was the real magic, Mistress Merrill knew that for sure. But just as The Flag seemed to lie still, the seagulls swooped down and rested on the old stone wall of the once proud home of a crofter and his family of long ago.

Mistress Merrill could sense a calm coming over the land thereabouts and looking round, she could see all kinds of animals gathering, looking at her, and at the two gnelfs who had lifted up the basket lid to look out.

She took the Flag of Leodhais and presented it to the surprised owner of the cottage, who accepted it gratefully and with a promise to give it a good place to rest. After nearly two hundred years, the Fairy Flag of Leodhais had truly come home at last.

Shipley had poked her head up out of her basket to see what was happening, and even though she was a cat, the smaller animals did not shy away; they knew they were safe. They were all safe now that *The Flag* had come home.

Mistress Merrill put Duncan and Isabella on the ground near the old cottage of The Flag; saying how she had enjoyed meeting with them, and that she would cherish the time they had spent together in returning the Fairy Flag of Leodhais.

The time had come, and without any fuss, she bid them farewell and rode off on her bicycle, with Shipley jumping and waving to the two gnelfs from her basket as the bicycle bounced along the grassy track back to the A866, the not-too-busy road of traffic to Steornabhagh.

Duncan and Isabella were on their own again, but this time they could sense that they were very near their new home. But which way should they go?

The weary Duncan and Isabella made their steady way along the grassy track in the same direction Merrill and Shipley had gone. After walking and stumbling for about a distance and a half, Duncan suggested they stop and climb on a nearby gatepost, to look out over the land, to see if they could see which way to go.

They both spotted the trees at the same time. It was a group of trees on the other side of the nearby stretch of water known as Broad Bay, a collection of trees the people of Leodhais called Bluewater Wood, in the Glen of Bluewater.

Duncan looked and looked again at the trees over the water of the bay, and he knew that was where they needed to be, that was where their new home would be.

A bheil thu 'g iarraidh orm do chuideachadh?
Uh, vil oo g.ee.urry orrom daw choojochugh?
Do you want me to help you?

Chapter 15
Time on a Beach and a Meeting with an Old Goat

The sun made the two little folk feel warm, and the breeze that was blowing them along the proper course made them easy of mind, as they float-walked closer and closer to what they thought would be their final destination. However, to Duncan's true regret, they did not seem to be getting any closer, and then he found out why…they were on a large beach, a wide and very long stretch of sand and pebbles.

The slopes of grass and trees of the hills of Steornabhagh on the island of Leodhais looked kindly welcoming to them when they had been with Merrill and Shipley.

Now, they were on the huge beach, those hills, trees, and grass were over there, over the bay, and further away across the noisy splashing waters.

It was just a wee bit of time-flicks later, and after wandering way out towards the sea, it seemed to the two gnelfs that the sandy, pebbly and windy beach they were on had become their new home. Not a nice thing to know, but at least, they had made it to their new world safely, and their life on the island could begin.

With the breeze playing with her curly hair, Isabella made a declaration, and one she was determined to keep, "If you think I have come all this way to live on sand and pebbles you are very much mistaken Duncan McTreggle. There is no way I am going to stay here, just no way."

Duncan's response was easy to understand, just, "Right, my dear…My dear one, we will find a way, trust me."

But first, they had to make it to the trees and grass, which they could see way off over the wide stretch of the beach of sand and pebbles; a wide seemingly barren land where no creatures could live, or so they thought.

…it takes time to take time…

92

With a warm gentle breeze pushing them this way and that, the two float-walking gnelfs moved carefully across the beach; making their way to the island hamlet of Tac Thunga, a village just to the north of Steornabhagh.

As they searched amongst the pebbles and sand for any sign of food, they breathed in the pleasant sea air of early evening time. Easy breathing in of good clean air gave them a good feeling inside and was a help in their float-walking, with Duncan leading the way towards Tac Thunga.

They were on the move to their new home, but as with most immigrants, and as Duncan and Isabella had already spotted before, they were to find their new home, certain obstacles would present themselves and would have to be dealt with.

Not more than 40 or 50 flicks of time later, they came to where Mother Nature had heaped up a part of the beach and made a large dune hill. It was a mixture of sand and pebbles that blocked their way forward and an obstacle that seemed to stretch away into the far distance on either side of them.

...but time will wait if you can wait with it...

Duncan tried to walk up the slope of the dune, but each time he gained three or four strides forward, and slightly up, he slid back down again in the soft sand and pebble mixture. He tried to float-walk up the slope but he did not have the skill, he could not manage float-walking up a hill, and neither could Isabella.

They were stuck out there on the seashore and a long way from the safety and comfort of the grass and heather hills of Leodhais.

If they could not go up and over, the only thing left for them to do was to do a long float-walk to their left or to their right, and Duncan was hungry.

"I don't like this, Izzy. It's not right for a gnelf to go hungry out here on the seashore, not right at all."

Isabella could not argue with him, it was not right, and she raised her voice in a declaration as if she could talk-shout the sand dune into giving in, "Oh, piffle, paffle, puffle, duffle, diffle…Not right at all!"

They stood at the bottom of the slope of sand and pebbles and wondered puzzled as to what to do for many flicks of time; too many flicks of time it seemed to Isabella.

Now, there was only one option as far as Duncan could fathom. There was no way they could go either left or right, it looked to be far too far, and they could be risking all kinds of unknown danger out on the open beach, it did not bear thinking about.

Then, not surprisingly, the one option that seemed to him was to climb up the slope of the sandy-pebbly dune hill using their hands and feet, one slow step-crawl at a time, and then slide down the other side.

With a quick nod to Isabella, and with a wave of a hand to indicate the slope, the two gnelfs began to climb up the hill in the old-fashioned, step-crawling way of hand over foot.

After a mighty struggle they managed to reach somewhere around a quarter way up the slope, and they sat themselves down amongst the dry sand and pebbles and looked back over the great region of flat beach they had passed through since leaving Merrill and Shipley.

They could just make out the waves of the sea running up and down the beach where they had thought their journey into a new life would begin and end.

It was amazing to them how they had managed to travel such a long way and in less than half a light-day.

"We've come a long way haven't we, Dunk'?" Isabella was a wee bit too tired to use her husband's full name.

She was even too tired to raise her voice to him when he failed to answer her question straight away.

Eventually, a certain few flicks of time later, Duncan answered, "I wonder if we've got much further to go…I am beginning to get a wee bit tired." As if to call attention to the fact, he yawned three times.

Then, just as he began his fourth yawn, Isabella, who had been watching his yawning technique with interest through half-closed eyes, looked up at the darkening sky, yawned her one and only yawn, and wriggled down into the sand and pebbles and went to sleep.

Two flicks of time, and one yawn later, Duncan had followed her example and he too had wriggled into the sandy and pebbles of the dune, and closed his eyes and gone to sleep.

Then, with the two of them snuggled down, the breeze seemed to caress the two little gnelfs as they wriggled slightly into the sloping hillside, with the breezy *umbrella* allowing Mr and Mrs McTreggle to sleep the happy sleep of contented gnelfs. Even the noise of the ever-watchful seagulls over the top of the beach and its dune hill did not stop them from going to sleep.

It was sometime later, when Duncan opened his eyes and shut them again, quickly. Then, as if in some kind of delayed response, with his mouth opening at the same time as he sat up, he shook his wife to wake her.

"Wa…Wass-up? I'm tired, can't you—"

Then she opened her eyes and asked a few questions:

"Oo-er! Dunky! What yer done?

The light-day is gone!

What's the lights-of-flashing?

What's that noise?

What's that rumbling?

Answer, will you?

What's going on, Duncan?"

Throughout the important moments of her fast flood of questions, the tired Mrs McTreggle stopped being tired, becoming more awake with each flick of time, and with each question she looked to her new loving and all-knowing husband for the reason why she was being bothered by *things*.

"I don't know!" his simple three-word reply was meant to be the answer to each one of the questions his wife had just asked him, and in all probability, would be used to answer the next question she was about to ask.

"What are you goin' to do, Dunky?"

They were both sitting up in a state of just-wakened-up shock. The seagulls had been screeching in their settling of the light-day chorus when the two gnelfs had closed their eyes and gone to sleep, snug and comfortable in the soft sandy bed. But now?

However, now there was no sunlight, it was night dark-cool, in fact, it was more than cool, it was *night-dark-cold*! Not only that but there were also weird, out-of-the-ordinary flashings of lights coming off a hill on the island at odd intervals.

Along with each flashing of lights coming from the top of the hill, there seemed to be a noisy bumbling movement coming from where the beach met the sea. They could also feel the sloping ground tremble beneath their feet when they stood up: they had felt it on their bottoms when they had first sat up. The ground was shaking, if only slightly, but it *was* definitely shaking.

Where there had been a wide-open beach there was the sea, and a slightly angry one it would seem. It had come in and crept up on them while they had been asleep, and the rumbling they could feel, and they could now see, was the waves crashing on the sand and pebbles at the bottom of the bank they were on.

Just a few flicks of wondering time later, after a quick escaping tumble out of their sandy and pebbly bed, and a roll down the slope, the two of them stood at the bottom of the sand dune again, not far from the water.

In the night dark of a moon-sky night, they were amazed at how the seawater had sneaked up on them.

Isabella asked another question, "What are we going to do, Duncan?"

He did not answer straight away, and while she waited for his answer Isabella looked around and made a statement that might have made her husband think harder, "I don't like it, Dunky, I don't like it at all."

The gnelf husband was not very keen on the situation either, but he would come to realise that it was one of those situations when it would be up to him. It was his time to be *The Elder*.

He would have to come up with a solution, and quick or being *The Elder* probably would not happen again for a long time.

"Now, look here, Izzy! There's no need to get in a miffle-muffle of a muddle, my dear, all we have to do is climb to the top of the sandy hill."

"*All?*" his wife's one-word question should have indicated that she might be just a little unsure of his solution. Even while considering that he was *The Elder*. *Duncan-the-Elder* continued, "All we have to do is get to the top and see what is on the other side, and see which way we have to go to our new world home."

Isabella was not at all sure about this, and a thought ran quickly through her mind. *It's alright for him to waffle on about getting to the top and deciding. But what if—*

Then, she attempted to put her thoughts into words, "Now, look here, yer—" But she was stumped for words, realising that there was probably nothing else for it if they were to move on, she would have to rely on he who was *The Elder*.

She would have to rely on her husband more than she had ever relied on anybody before. He would definitely have to be *The Elder* and a good one at that.

Duncan stood tall, *(well, tallish,)* and wriggled his shoulders, with his ears doing the same.

He then took Isabella's hand, and as their fingers entwined he spoke calmly, quietly and slowly, "I know we've never come across anything like this afore, Izzy, but I think if we help each other, and try and keep real calm, we will be just fine, you'll see!"

In all the little time she had known her husband, Isabella had never heard him speak like it before, in fact, she had never heard anyone speak like it before.

It was as if her husband had suddenly changed into a wise and strong, and yet so gentle *Elder of the Gnelfs*. Little did she know, or he for that matter, that there would be times when they would both have to be *The Elder*, and that there would be many future secrets for both of them to discover about each other, and their new world.

The climb up the steep slope of the hilly sandbank, in the dark, turned out to be a wee bit more awkward than it was in a light-day, but it seemed that all they had to do was take their time, treading softly, and carefully help each other as they made their way up, one easy step at a time.

Some struggling flicks of time later; as they came to the top of the *mountain* of sand and pebbles and looked down the other side—which was a lot steeper than the side they had just climbed, Duncan considered.

Him still being *The Elder*, he turned to speak with Isabella, his voice raised slightly, "Now, my dear, it would seem that we have only one option open to us, we—"

Isabella did not let him finish what he was saying, and, shouting louder than he had been shouting, she told him, "Never mind, it would seem! And stop calling me your *deer*. If you think I am going to go down there here, you must be crazier than any dimfy-dunce we have ever known!"

Not waiting for an answer, she pulled her husband away from the top of the *mountain* and dragged him down the slope of the hill a wee bit, then, letting go of her grip on his sweaty sandy hand, she stamped her feet and sank up to her knees in the loose sand and pebble mix beneath her. But she ignored the pickle she was in and placed her hands on her hips to make a public statement.

"You great big *neaming stit*! *(I think she meant to say* steaming nit*)* Are you out of your mind? If we didna' get scratched and squished, we would probably die of fright for not being scratched and squished…Of all the pea-brained ideas, this one takes the acorn.

"When and how are we going to…may I ask? Do you reckon we are to perform this miracle of climbing down the cliff o' loss, eh? The mad thing, eh? Or are we just going to leave it to luck and float-walk our way down?"

Then, with a slight hint of mockery in her voice, she ended with, "But then! You never know, as we float-walk our way down, we might just manage to miss the bottom and land on a bed of feathers, and sit up smelling of heather and honey and…and…and the like."

Duncan breathed slow and easy while his wife had *discussed* matters with him. Then, as she brought those *matters* to a close, he took a couple of good gulps of air and lifted to a good knee height, so that when he spoke he talked to the top of her head.

"Now, then, my dear, if you will let me finish! I was saying that we will have to go down the other side, *in the morning of light-day!*" he shouted the last part of his statement in a loud and strict fashion.

Isabella spoke calmly and lovingly. "There's no need for you to be shouting at me, Duncan McTreggle, you could have just told me…I would have understood—"

Waiting for his wife to finish talking, Duncan opened his lips slightly, blew out gently, and came back down to the sloping sand and pebbles of the side of the hill and back down the way they had just struggled. But then, forgetting that he was on a slope, the overconfident gnelf lost his balance and tippled over, and just as nature intended it would seem.

He tumbled on down the slope and he didn't stop tumbling until he met accidentally with a grumbling and mumbling old smelly goat, who had sat down by the seawater for a moment to rest, and look out to sea and have a think. A long slow think in the cooling sea breeze.

Duncan rolled up against the goat's back with a thump, just at the part where the tail fits.

The rolling-gnelf apologised as the goat sat up, "Oops! I'm sorry…Mr Goat. Sir! But I've just come down from up there." Duncan pointed up at the top of the sandy-pebbly hill.

"And what were you a doin' up there on *sandy-pebbly mountain* then, my little roller? Were you after gettin' over and down yon side, eh?" the old goat talked through his gruff mumbling and grumbling while his two big front feet, which were hoofed and hard, scratched at the sandy, pebbly ground as if he was intent on keeping his hooves even harder than they were.

Duncan looked at the goat right in the eye, the one nearest to him that is, and asked an important question, "Mr Goat Sir, my name is Duncan McTreggle, and I am asking, can you tell me how do *you* get over this here hill on your night dark walkabouts?"

Mr Goat did not answer straight away, he just started to scratch at his tummy with one of his back feet, and then, after a good last scratch, he stopped scratching and looked up the sand and pebble-covered slope, with both of his eyes fixed on the downward moving figure of Isabella McTreggle.

He waited, with his grumbling easing down to just a crotchety murmur while Isabella came rolling down to join Duncan at the goat's tail, where the little lady gnelf and her husband sat together.

Looking over his shoulder, *Mr Goat* talked to the both of them, "Now then, my Dears, my name is Old Goat, and I've got something to show you…Come with me will you?"

Duncan introduced himself and Izzy to Old Goat as they followed him.

It was probably because he was feeling the importance of his island knowledge, but when he spoke again his voice *bleated* slightly.

Despite the occasional whooshing noise coming from the sea, his bleating, "Come with me, will you?" seemed to echo around the otherwise quiet beach.

Then the three of them made their way along a narrow footpath that followed the bottom of the hill of sand and pebbles, and Old Goat began to sing one of his *bleating songs*. To him, it was a *goaty* melody, but to others, it was a complaining noise only:

We live together in the woods and heather.
We live in the hills where it is all good.
We live on the sand and pebbly beach,
We share the day.
We share the night.
We make the everything-thing just right,
All in a breath togetherer—
(Togetherer?)

A singing goat is a rare thing indeed, and, not surprisingly, the bleating song attracted some spectators, with a few rabbits hopping along the top of the dune to see what was going on—but, they soon left when Brush Tail Fox appeared on the scene.

A Hoot Owl swooped in quietly, to sit perfectly still on the top of a nearby bit of a sunken boat post, watching and missing nothing with wide staring eyes.

Other smaller creatures were there too, but they kept out of sight. It just would not do for one of them to get in the way of Old Goat; he could be a mite careless with those hard hooves of his at times, and there *was* Hoot Owl and Brush Tail Fox to consider.

Even so, it was a rare treat for all of those who were within hearing range of the *bleating-singing;* a treat that they would all remember fondly, including the two gnelfs.

Then the singing stopped, and Old Goat spoke to the McTreggles calmly and easily, "Here you are, my Dears!" He pointed his bearded chin towards something in the bank of the sandy, pebbly dune. "This is where you and I can cross without fault or favour, in dry or wet."

Author's Note:
What he meant by fault or favour *escapes me, but that is goat-speak for you.*

Looking in the direction Old Goat's chin had indicated, Duncan and Isabella could see what looked like the entrance to a cave, a small cave, and one that seemed to disappear into the slope of sand and pebbles.

"But it's just a cave!" Isabella's way of speaking did seem to indicate the disappointment she was feeling.

Old Goat looked at her with his left eye; snuffled and grumbled a bit. Then, he put her straight.

Looking at Isabella with both of his eyes and pushing his wet snout close to her face, he said, "No! It isna a cave, it's tunnel pipe, a tunnel pipe that runs under the sandy hill clear through to the other side, my dear."

Isabella looked at the goat carefully and came to the conclusion that the Old Goat was cross-eyed as she realised he was looking somewhere over her shoulder, while at the same time talking to her as if indeed she *was* somewhere over her own shoulder.

As she listened to Old Goat and watched his eyes, the lady gnelf could not help but wonder how a cross-eyed old goat could help them find their new home, he probably had a job in finding his own.

Duncan stepped up to the tunnel pipe entrance and peered into its dark round interior.

"Eh! Look Isabella…Look! It does go through! I can see the other side outside on."

Author's Note:
I had to puzzle about that, but I think I know what he meant.

Not wishing to waste much of his precious time, Old Goat push-nudged Duncan to one side and grumbled, "Come on, follow Old Goat, he will show you the way…Come on!"

Feeling a wee bit happier; even though following a goat in the small tunnel pipe was a real smelly business, the two gnelfs took regular gulps of air and float-walked after Old Goat. By keeping their feet just above the odd puddles of water that were along the tunnel floor; and by flapping their hands slowly, they managed to float-walk their way to the other side of the *sandy-pebbly mountain*, with Old Goat scuffling and shuffling along in front of them.

All gentlemen and lady gnelfs are a lot stronger than their wee size would indicate, and when it comes to stone-throwing, there are none finer, or further.

Chapter 16
Isabella the Stone Thrower (Part 1)

After saying farewell to Old Goat, the tired and weary Duncan and Isabella eventually found a nice warm spot in some long grass near a tree, close to the hamlet of Tac Thunga, and spent a good, proper night as immigrant gnelfs above ground, under the low-hanging branches of a tree.

Their journey from a settled gnome and elf underground world in Blackwater Forest on the Isle of Arran had not exactly been easy, but at least it had been interesting. Now, they could sleep the sleep of the tired and weary, and think on about their travels with their journey nearly over, their thoughts on what their new home will look like.

'I'm only little me, after all,' Marlow Mulzie.

The Second Day on the Isle of Leodhais.

It was light-day beginning number two on the island, and the two gnelfs had not yet found their new home, and this concerned Mrs Isabella McTreggle greatly, a fact of life she intended to inform her husband about.

"Duncan!" She exclaimed her husband's name but nicely, even though it was a question really. Then she repeated herself, in a more questioning fashion.

"Duncan?" Then, she did it again, a bit louder and more forcefully. "*Duncan McTreggle?*"

Then, it was Duncan's turn to ask a question, in a quieter voice, "Yes, my dear?"

Then there came another, quieter question from Mrs McTreggle, "What do you mean by 'yes, my dear', eh?"

Duncan thought for a flick or two and then gave a simple reply, "Well, you did say my name!"

Then, he straight away followed with another question, "What did you say it for?"

Isabella could see where this was going, and if she did not put a stop to it, they would be in a question-to-question mix-up.

"Now listen, Dunky, stop asking question-questions, and just listen, will you?"

(Now that was not a question)
Duncan got ready to listen.
Isabella spoke, "Duncan?"
(Oh Dear, not another question!)

Realising her mistake, Isabella calmly and skilfully moved away from the questioning way of things, "My good Duncan, it seems to me that we do not know how far it is to our new home." She looked at her husband to check that he was still listening, and continued, nicely, "We only know that our new world home is somewhere on this island of Leodhais, and even though we do not know where it is or what it is called, we need to work things out a wee bit don't you think? So, to help us work things out a bit, I think we should have something to eat now, and then—"

However, Duncan was not listening anymore; with Isabella having mentioned the act of eating, his mind had wandered over to the subject of food, and he was beginning to look around for the nearest morsel.

"*And then*!" Isabella shouted a two-word statement and made it more important in listening value by the simple use of a good push on the shoulder of her hungry husband.

Duncan leaned to one side, tottered a little, and then paid attention to his wife.

Isabella continued, "And then, I think we should find a way to make it easier for ourselves and look for something to guide us."

Duncan's attention perked up a lot, and he gave it some excited thought.

What a great idea! The thought moved swiftly across his mind, and he just could not help himself. "Isabella! You're not just my wife, you are a genoose! *(I think he meant* genius.*)* We should go and find Shipley, or Mistress Merrill, or Old Goat perhaps, yes?"

Isabella did not answer her wondering husband, but without waiting for any more guiding ideas from Izzy, Duncan looked around in the gathering bright of the new light-day, trying his best to locate something; anything, some item or other that he might give them a chance, which might be a guide.

He did not see it right away; his head was below the grass level, but parked just a wee bit down the lane towards the village was a butcher's bicycle. It was one with a basket on the front, and it was lying on the ground with its basket on the grassy bank near the butcher's shop.

It was going to be easy, all they had to do was get to the bicycle and find a nice easy secretive spot in the basket.

This should be easy-peasy, thought Duncan.

Meanwhile, Isabella had been busy collecting food for their planned meal, confident that having come up with the idea, she could leave the rest to her husband; after all, that's what husbands are for in the new world of the gnelfs.

She was sure that Duncan would find them a guide.

He had! If only they could get to it in time.

Isabella placed her collection of food on the ground and spoke to him nicely, and then listened while her husband explained.

Then, it was her turn to speak again, "That's clever of you, Dunky." Her voice was soft and tinkly in a very pleasant bell-like sounding sort of way, and it remained so as she continued, "Do you want me to help you?"

Trying hard not to bob about too much, Duncan lifted his arm very slowly while moving closer to the waiting bicycle and its basket. He then put his arm back down again while Izzy hung on to him, with the both of them slowly breathing out.

"*Duncan!* Just let your breath out, and give me your arm, I'll grab hold of it. It will be easy, you'll see, come on."

Duncan raised his arm again and continued to breathe out, dropping slowly down to the ground as he did so.

"It's alright, Dunky, we can do it."

And they did! With Duncan already bending his knees, Isabella lowered herself slightly, and together they took a deep breath in and leapt into the basket. With the pleasing result that not many flicks later, they were both sitting safely in the bottom corner of the basket on the butcher's bicycle.

Isabella looked at her husband straight in the eyes. "What it is…What it means is that we can now get to our new world easily, just by sitting here and waiting, eh, Dunky? Then down the lane in our basket to our new home!"

A few flicks of time flicked by as the two of them considered options, with Duncan thinking that his wife's statement really did need a comment from him, and, surprising himself, he suddenly thought of one.

Talking in the manner of a Gnelf Elder, he made a statement, "I think we should forget this basket idea thing, Isabella." He had worked out that if the bicycle went the opposite way they could be taken further from their new home. "It might take us longer, but—" Sadly, he could not think of how to finish, and he stopped talking.

Mrs Isabella McTreggle was not very pleased with her husband's non-talking response to her statement. As far as she was concerned float-walking was easy for short distances; *tiny,* short distances that is, but they didn't know how far they still had to go before they found their new home. What's more, she did not want to spend sleep-time in the long grass that collected soggy wet dew.

No, and definitely no, she wasn't going to give in that easy, and she was determined to make her husband see that by letting the bicycle take the basket, and the basket to take them, they would find a new home place that bit sooner.

"Now, look here, husband of mine, if you want to wear yourself out flapping your hands while you puff and breathe, *(I think she meant breathe in and out fast)* then, get on with it, I'm not giving up."

It was thinking time, but poor little Duncan could not think the right way around; his mind had gone into a blank dip, and he had an ache-head. It was no good, he would have to put his head somewhere quiet and cool until the ache-head left him.

"Sorry, Izzy. I'll have to go and find a bushy bush, I've got a thumping ache-head."

Isabella's voice was a long way from tinkly as she answered by making her feelings known. "Sorry! You've got a nerve, Dunky. Sorry! You'll get sorry. How am I going to work it out on my own? Eh?"

Poor Duncan, he was nearly fainting with the thump, thump, thump, thump of his ache-head. It was all he could manage to roll out of the basket and totter over to the welcome coolness of the underside of a nearby bush, and push his head into the cool comforting tickle of the soft green leaves hanging down from its lower branches. Then, with his aching head still thumping, he sat down on the soft crumbly soil under the bush to wait for the ache-head to go away. There was just nothing else he could do.

Isabella stood up in the basket and cursed her way around the woven interior in circles. "Puffle, chuffle, puffle, suffle, tuffle, wuffle, duffle, chuffle." And so on, with her feet stamping out the words on the side of the basket in a simple rhythm, while her clenched hands, punched up in the air on each side of her as she stomped.

Then she paused, and with her eyes open wide, her hands came unclenched and she sat perfectly still, then, within a few flicks of time, she lost her glaring expression, looked in her husband's direction more kindly, and shouted, "Duncan! I know how we can do it!"

"Err…Mmmmmm…go…away," was all the response she got, her husband's voice muffled as it was by the leafy hospital bush.

But Isabella was determined. "Oh! Alright, I'll do it on my *own*!" And as if to show how determined she was, she gave one last stomp of her right foot as she said *own*.

Mrs McTreggle did not waste any time. She knew it was up to her, and she would see that whatever needed doing would be done.

If anyone could have seen her, they would have thought her to be a really brave lady gnelf, a daft brave gnelf maybe, but a brave one just the same. We have to understand that it could not have been an easy decision for her, but she did not hang about in making her mind up to get on with it.

Wasting no time, Isabella dropped out of the basket and found a small stone, a round and pebbly one like those on the beach. Gripping the pea-sized stone in her hand, she flung her arm back and then threw the stone as far as she could up the lane out of the village.

Duncan tried to argue that his aching head was hurting him and that he needed to be alone, but Isabella would not have any of it. "Come on, Dunky, I have found a way for us to find our new home. Help me to find it, my dear and you can then rest as much as you like…Please?"

It was the *please* that probably did it, or maybe the promise of never-ending rest, but whatever it was, Duncan with the aching head bravely crawled out of the cool bush and stood by the side of his dear wife.

"All we have to do, Dunky, is follow the stone!"

"What stone?"

"The stone I have just thrown along the road."

Duncan was gobsmacked, with his mouth open.

Isabella could see that her ache-head of a husband needed to be convinced.

"You see, Dunky, my dear, the stone will show us the way like the Flag did, even when it was just a Cloth. Wherever it goes we follow, it's so easy, don't you see?"

Now our Duncan is sometimes a wee bit slow on the uptake, but on this occasion, he was right on the ball.

"But you are the one who is throwing it, Izzy."

"That has nothing whatsoever to do with it, I might be the one that throws it, but it is the stone that is going in the direction we can follow."

Isabella had convinced herself that she was right, and no matter what Duncan said or did there was no changing that; they would definitely be following the stone.

'Se oidhche mhath bha sin
seh uh-eech-yuh va uh va shin
That was a lovely evening.

Chapter 17
Isabella the Stone Thrower (Part 2)

Author's Note:

I dare say, you have worked it out for yourself. What Isabella was doing was just getting her own way; the stone-throwing was just a cover-up. However, even if Duncan did see through her method, they carried on together.

Four stone throws later found them by a stream, a wide and slow-flowing stream, which seemed to be going in the direction the stone was indicating. Then, on the sixth throw, they came to a small wooden plank-boat that appeared to be stuck at the edge of the stream.

Delicately they went on.

Author's Note:

From what Duncan told me I would reckon that their plank-boat, as he called it, was just a small plank of wood.

As they pondered on what to do, Duncan said he had begun another ache-head, and he went off to find a hospital bush to go under and cool off.

In the meantime, pulling up her heavy skirt, Isabella sat down on the plank-boat at the edge of the stream, with her legs over the side, her feet just dangling in the water. This was it, this was when it could be. Duncan or no Duncan, this was it. This was…

"Aw get on with it, Isabella McTreggle!" she shouted the words at herself.

Gripping hold of a couple of tufts of stubby grass on the bank edge and letting the hem of her skirt fall where it may, Isabella slowly and very gently, and bit by bit, let herself and the plank-boat slide away from the bank and out onto the water. Then the boat suddenly caught the flow of the stream.

It was horrible, and just as she was about to scream her husband's name, the boat bumped lightly into the pebbles on the bottom of the stream, and she softly squeaked, "Duncan!"

After lifting her legs out of the water, and putting both of her feet on the boat, Isabella lifted her head as high as she could and placed her hands on the wet flat surface of the plank-boat as it followed the flow of the water, with the *captain* and only passenger facing the wrong way.

Looking across at the bank, watching it changing as she floated her way down the stream on her new flat plank-boat, Isabella considered steering it to the bank somehow, to wait for her husband. But it would be easier if he was there to help her. But it would seem that she would have to hang about until his ache-head had gone, but then she remembered that ache-heads sometimes take a long time to go.

"Oh bother!" she whispered to herself. "I can't wait around for his ache-head to go. I will have to do it by myself. I'll just have to behave properly and safely." She paused for a flick of time or two as she looked around, and then she whispered to herself again, "And I won't know if I can do it till I try."

Isabella finally made her decision, and with a great struggle, she managed to stand up and turn round to face in the right direction. She quickly learned how to guide the plank-boat by leaning one way or the other as it wobbled in the flow of the water, and the plank-boat and its ex-stone-throwing passenger/captain sailed off down the stream to who knows where.

Author's Note:

The lady gnelfs of Steornabhagh wear green tunics and heavy green skirts, and no hat (except for weddings) and on their feet they wear thick green pointed boots made from the leaves of ash trees; boots that flop about when wet.

Chapter 18
Captain Isabella Mctreggle

Being the captain of a boat was fine, or so thought Mrs McTreggle, as the plank of a boat she happened to be the captain of, levelled off and settled on the smooth watery flow; with the gently flowing water of the stream taking her where she wanted to go with hardly any effort at all on her part.

Then, she thought of Duncan, and she realised; in a flick of time, that the future wouldn't be all that great for herself and her husband if she carried on without him. Especially with her being the captain of a plank-boat without a crew, and he with his head stuck in a bush.

...and on...

It was a make-your-mind-up sort of state of affairs for Isabella as she thought that things could not get much worse, but then, thinking again and very quickly, she decided that maybe they could. Anyway, what could she do? She might be the captain of the plank-boat, but there was no way she was going to turn it around and head back upstream. She couldn't do that even if she wanted to, she just didn't know how!

Floating nicely and very safely, the plank-boat continued to take her steadily further away from her husband, while her mind mixed with the thoughts of what she could or should do. She could stay on the plank-boat as captain and passenger, to make her own boating way to the new home world and leave her husband to find her later. Or she could somehow get the plank-boat to the bank and leave it there, while she went back for her husband.

On the other hand, she could resort to.

"Huffle, puffle, ruffle, gruffle, tuffle, wuffle and him and his ache-heads!" *(Heads?)*

She was going to stamp her foot but then thought better of it. It was not a sensible thing to do on a small plank of a boat out on the water. Therefore, she just turned her head to look back in the direction of where she had last seen her husband; which meant she did not bother to look where she and the plank-boat were going. *(Oh dear, she really should have looked.)*

With her back to the way she and the plank-boat were going and while she was still *huffling and ruffling*, Isabella's tunic collar came in contact with the wet thin end of a low-hanging twiggy branch of a tree that; not many flicks of time before, had been trapped under the water, held there by a boulder.

But Isabella's plank-boat had nudged the boulder and rolled it over ever so slightly to one side, with the result that the branch had suddenly become free from being held down by the boulder, to shoot up towards the sky in a slow whipping action.

As it whipped upwards, the thin end of the branch picked up *Captain* Mrs McTreggle by the collar, with the result that the *first lady gnelf* was hanging on for dear life, to the thin wet end of the branch firmly lodged under her tunic collar as she and the branch shot skyward. Then, after only a couple of flicks of time, *Captain* Isabella found herself on the bank.

Well, she was not exactly on the bank, although she *was* out of the water. Her connection with the bank was from more than halfway up a tall beech tree of great age, which, as far as Isabella was concerned, was also of great height. And seeing that she was right in the middle of it, and nearly at the top, it did mean that she was a long, long way from the ground.

Now, here is a pickle. The plank-boat was floating steadily down the stream and on towards the new home world.

While high in the treetops, the *captain* Mrs Isabella McTreggle, sat swinging her legs, and muttering, "piffle, paffle, puffle." And banging her hands on her knees each time she said one of her *words*.

...steady as you go...

However, the sad feature of the completely sorry state of things was the kilted rear of her husband still sticking out from under the green leafy bush. What is more, he should have been the one and only member of her crew aboard the plank-boat; the very boat that was sailing off to the new home world without a captain or crew.

In the leafy height of the old tree not far away from the stream, Isabella was thinking aloud again. "I blame myself. I should have…No, I should not have listened to that pea-wit-brained husband of mine…It is his entire fault—

"If it was not for him making an ache-head for himself, I wouldna be up here now! I dunna know! Why couldn't he just get a cold head or ache-tooth? Oh no! Just like a man gnelf when you need him most, he has to have an ache-head…I hope his ache-head is a thumpity, thumpity one, it would serve him right."

(Now, then Isabella, that is not nice at all.)
…steady, and even further on…

While the first lady gnelf had been saying her thoughts out loud, a cool breeze had begun to blow on the nasty-tempered tree-sitter. Then, it began to blow a bit stronger, and then a bit more, and Isabella calmed down a little. She didn't like the way the wind was making the tree shake as she realised that her difficult position was getting even more difficult.

Further upstream, on the bank, the kilted rounded rear end of Duncan McTreggle moved slightly in the cooling breeze, and then a long deep sigh could be heard coming from under the leafy bush where the rest of Mr McTreggle was positioned.

Then, wonder of wonders, the whole of the green-clad figure of Mrs McTreggle's husband stumbled out from under the cool shelter of the leafy hospital bush.

His ache-head had gone, and the gentle fluttering strokes of the green leaves and the cool ground had done the trick. In fact, he felt positively fiddling-fit and healthy, and he looked around to speak to his wife but spoke to himself instead, "Where is she? I don't know! I turn me back for a few flicks of time, and what do you know; she's gone and left me, deserted me—"

Author's Note:
There was a distinct possibility of an ache-head making an early return if he was not careful.

"Steady, Dunky. Keep nice and calm," he said to himself. "She won't be far away!"

Then, taking a good look around, Duncan decided that Isabella must have continued and gone in search of their new home world without him. So, taking a long slow intake of breath, he float-walked slowly along the path by the stream, keeping to the short grass where he could, and going in the general direction of the water flow downstream.

He was correct, his dear wife *had* continued. But she had then been made to pause, and after just a few flicks of time Duncan was made aware of this pause, and the fact that his wife was close by when a voice from above proclaimed, "Eh you! Beetle brain, it is your fault. You did this to me!"

Hardly daring to look up, Duncan let out his breath to allow his body to drop back down to the ground, and putting one hand on his forehead, just where the ache-head had been, he tilted his head back bit by bit, until it was right back. Oh! What a sight. He had seen his wife's feet before, but surely, they were not that big!

He found it hard not to think about feet, never mind mention them.

However, holding himself in check, he muttered a few words of wisdom to himself, "Hold on, Duncan, keep right calm and nice, don't you get carried away."

Then, ignoring the feet and taking charge of the situation, he shouted up at Isabella, well, her feet really, "Hold on, Izzy, keep calm. I will get you down soon." He had been doing fine, right up to the word *soon*.

"*Soon!* You'll get *soon!* You had better be getting me down now—" His wife made her thoughts on the matter very clear to him, as per usual.

Realising his spoken error, Duncan then began to elaborate on his unfortunate choice of word. "Yes, dear. Now, when I said soon, I really meant that I would not be long. It was just my way of saying that if everything goes according to plan—"

He paused for a few time-flicks, and thought, *What plan? I haven't got a plan!*

Ignoring his unhelpful thoughts, he carried on with his verbal communication with his highly positioned wife, "If everything goes according to plan, you'll be down here with me in a few flicks—before you know it in fact."

The voice from above expressed an opinion, "*Plan! What plan?*"

Then events took a surprising turn for the better. *(Depending on how you look at it.)*

The thin branch Isabella was sitting on began to droop. It could not continue to withstand the blustery wind and a bouncing and knee-slapping lady gnelf; even though she was small in the normal way of things. And the situation hasn't helped any by the lady in question trying to show how upset she was by placing both hands on the branch and shaking it.

Creek. The sticking-out normal state of the branch began to change to a more down-sloping curve and one that put the end of it back closer to the ground.

Changing her position slightly, Isabella went quiet and lost all interest in what her husband's *plan* might be, and she started to slide ever so gently, at first.

Crack! Scramble! Crunchle! Crinkle! Bongle! Trumble! Squiggle…THUMP! *The lady of the tree* had landed, and after doing so, she gave way to her deepest feelings.

"Piffle, tiffle, waffle, giffle, riffle, liffle, baffle," and so it went on, for a good many flicks of time.

Then she realised she was at least safe on the ground again, and the cursing stopped.

Duncan stayed calm and just watched as his wife ruffled at her dark brown hair, pulled a lot of thorns from her skirt and tunic, and rubbed her knees. pressed her skirt gently down the back of her legs, and then kicked the huge trunk of the innocent tree.

Mr Duncan McTreggle braced himself for the expected curses that could be put on him.

However, he was pleased to note that his wife had ceased her cursing, and was brushing lightly at the sides of her skirt, and turning round to face him…To cry.

Isabella's feelings were all mixed up: her knees were hurting, her bottom was bruised, she was sure. She loved her pee-wit-brained husband to bits, and she felt the need to have a good old-fashioned cry.

Duncan took his wife in his arms and stroked her hair when she put her head on his shoulders and said nothing, and neither did Duncan, while he waited for her to rid herself of the shock she had suffered from falling down from a tall tree.

They had lost all sense of time; and the plank-boat as well, and they were more tired than they had realised. So, it wasn't much of a surprise to either of them that when they lay down together in the long grass and cuddled up with their arms wrapped around each other, they went to sleep then and there.

Author's Note:
1. *What the two gnelfs did not know was that they were home; they had made it to their new world home in Bluewater Wood in Bluewater Glen.*
2. *All gnelfs are vegetarian and they can talk with any creature and, oddly, they know the language of all plants.*

They knew they were close to the end of their journey, all about them was softly greeting them to a new homeland. All they needed to do was to find where they were going to settle down. Where their new home would be.

'Waste not time debating on what a good person should do, just be one.'
With thanks to Marcus Aurelius Roman Emperor. 121-180 AD

Chapter 19
Ben Old

Not far from where the two gnelfs lay asleep in the long grass by the stream, there stood a woodsman's cottage; one that belonged to Ben, an old man who had looked after Bluewater Wood, and other parts of Bluewater Glen, all his working life.

If truth be told, he had also helped to look after things around the cottage, even before he had been big enough to do a day's work, helping his father and mother when he was just a boy no more than five or six years of age.

However, since he had become an old man and did not have a son or a daughter of his own to help him, there wasn't much he could do. He just did a wee bit of tidying up here and there, keeping the paths clear of tall grass and weeds, or clipping back a few scrambling-tangling branches of bushes.

And also helped some of the less fortunate creatures he came across that had hurt themselves or, like him, had become a bit too old. In fact, overall, he did not do too badly for an old man on his own, and Bluewater Wood and its animals and plants were better off for him being there.

It was a good evening, in kind spring weather, the season being a warm one for a change, and the old man had decided to take a walk down the field path, to the bridge over the stream just two fields down from his cottage.

He would then take the path that was just over on the other side of the bridge, with his intention being to walk by the stream and follow it as far as the bottom of Bluewater Wood, where the trees of the wood grew on each side of the stream.

Not one for wasting an opportunity, Ben had taken his grass-cutting tool along with him; a sharp curved bladed tool with a handgrip, a tool that could cut grass in a whisper of action.

Just after crossing over the wooden bridge that all local folk knew as *The Auld Bridge*, the old woodsman spotted a clump of grass and weeds growing over the path and nearly hiding the pathway altogether. Now, that would not do! He was not going to have that.

Taking the sharp curved metal grass-cutting tool out of its leather cover, he walked calmly and quietly up to the offending clump of grass and weeds.

Now, don't you go thinking that the old woodsman just cut things down willy-nilly. No, far from it, he had never taken to destroying what Mother Nature had slowly but surely attended to, especially natural wild growing things. But there were times when it just had to be done, and as he stood looking at the straggling and gangly grass and weeds growing over the path, he decided that this was one of those times.

The chattering, whistling and chirping of birds were noises that the old woodsman of Bluewater Wood had lived with all his life. He had heard it so often that he had long since taken it for granted, sounds that had been part of his days, and nights, for years.

But when he swung his arm back at that moment in time with the sharp metal-bladed tool gripped tight in his fisted hand, that part of Bluewater Glen around him became silent. The silence made him go cold, and he held the grass and weed cutter behind his back, to give him time to check things out.

He looked around slowly and spotted a number of birds just perched; *sitting* without making a sound, and watching him.

"Well, I never," he said to himself. "I've ne'er seen the like afore!"

He was amazed. It was a kind of magical. It was as if the birds knew that there was something there in that clump of grass and weeds he was about to cut down. That must be why they had gone quiet.

"Well, if that be true," he was still talking to himself, and he repeated his words a wee bit louder as if trying to inform the wildlife around him. "Well, if that be true…I'll put me grass and weed cutter down an' not bother with it."

As soon as he had put the sharp metal tool down on the ground, the birds straight away began their singing, whistling and chirping, and or so, it seemed to the old woodsman, the glen thereabouts sort of came back to normal natural and happy sounding life again.

Rubbing his whiskery chin and looking at the clump of grass and weeds, he listened to the birds, and from the way they had been behaving, he knew he would have to move carefully if he was to find out what it was that had made them go so quiet.

All the same, that would be no problem for the old man, moving carefully was second nature to him. There was no one more careful than Ben the old woodsman.

He moved slowly, intending to lean over the clump of grass and weeds that were not more than a couple of steps away from him. It was a wonder that he had not disturbed whatever was there before he had even moved towards the spot. Either it or *they* were very tired or deaf, if they had not heard him as he had come along by the stream; with his booted feet rustling through the grasses and weeds that were close by the path.

Putting his feet down slowly and gently, the old woodsman moved forward. Then, when he was right up close, he bent himself over a wee bit and peered down with his elderly eyes, trying his best to look through the tops of the grass and weed growth to see what lay in hiding underneath.

Being very cautious, and using both hands gently, he moved the grass and weed tops aside slowly, treating them as if they were feathers… and got the surprise of his long life.

Boy oh boy! He had always sort of known there were such things as gnomes, elves and fairies in Bluewater Wood and Bluewater Glen, he'd never doubted it one bit, but now, by jiminy! Now, there they were, right in front of his eyes, so close, he could have touched them, and it was all he could do to stop himself from crying out.

Nevertheless, and even though his old, wrinkled face was set in a happy grinning fashion, his eyes started to water with the beginning of tears. The two little *gnomes* or that's what the old woodsman thought them to be, they looked so perfect and gently lying in each others' arms, so content and happy together in a quiet sleep.

I'll leave 'em, he thought, *it wouldn't be right to wake 'em, an' maybe upset 'em—it would frighten ''em*, and with this thought on his mind, he wiped his shirt sleeve over his eyes.

Not wishing to hurt, or alarm the little folk, the old chap began to lean away. But as he did, his old back seemed to creak and he felt a sharp twinge of pain, and he couldn't stop himself from giving a murmur of a grunt. And, even though, he kept his mouth tight shut, the noise he made was enough to disturb the two sleeping little folk.

…to sleep is to dream, sort of…

"Who? Wha'? Duncan! Are you awake? Was that you grunting?" The lady of the two little sleepers was just opening her eyes. She wasn't sure what it was she had heard, what it was that had awakened her. *Had she been dreaming?*

As she asked her husband the questions she was shaking his shoulder, and while doing so she looked up. To see the wrinkled human whiskery face looking down at them.

"Duncan*! Duncan?*"

"Whaa'?" it was one drawn-out word of a question, asked by an eyes-closed soon-to-be *Elder of the Gnelfs of Bluewater Wood*. Then, he opened his eyes. "Aye? Who? What?"

Thanks to the old woodsman's creaky old back, introductions would have to be made.

The old chap could not believe it; just the sight of the two *gnomes (he would know them to be gnelfs later)* made him feel as if he was a young boy again. As a young boy, he could only guess how the gnomes and fairies of *his* Bluewater Wood lived; with him often wondering at the things they got up to, and the happy times they must have in the secret parts of the wood and glen.

It had been a good, honest and happy way to be a youngster in those far-off days; in a time, when it was accepted that it was your right to be that way—if you so wished. Now, right now, right here before his eyes, was the living and breathing proof that little folk do live in Bluewater Glen, and maybe, even in Bluewater Wood.

The old woodsman dropped down onto his knees as gently as he could, ignoring his creaking and aching back, and the sharp stabs of pain in his knees, to speak gently and softly to the little creature who sat up while rubbing at her tiny gnelf eyes.

"Now then, my dear, don't you go a frettin' yourself none. I'm not going to harm you," he whispered the words, hardly opening his mouth as he did so, and the birds thereabouts seemed to stop their twittering for a moment, as if, they were trying to listen in to what he was saying.

Isabella stopped rubbing her eyes and sat up straighter. *That wasn't Duncan's voice.*

In fact, it wasn't like any voice she had heard before. Then she looked up again.

"Piffle, waffle, taffle, graffle, shaffle, daffle, naffle!" Then she stopped her cursing and just sat with her mouth open, waiting for her husband to wake up a bit more.

But all she got was, "Whaa'! What are you cursing for? What's up now? Can't I be left alone? To sleep, eh?"

Isabella shook her husband by the shoulder again, and much harder than before. "Dunky! Wake up its…It's…It's!" She could not say it; she could not bring herself to say it was an old human, and that he was talking to her.

"Duncan McTreggle, you…Puffle, tuffle, gruffle, wuffle, suffle!"

Duncan turned on his back, sat up, and then looked up. Then, he sat up a bit more, looked up a bit more, and said a few words that formed a collection of questions, "What the? Who? Eh? Away with you, you are not supposed to see us. Go away, and pretend you haven't seen us will you?"

Then, having said his say, and being *The Elder* again, Duncan stopped talking and looked at his wife and thought, *What am I doing? I am talking to a human… I shouldn't be doing this at all.*

He then, went back to talking to himself, "Steady, Dunc, keep calm, take a few deep breaths."

Yes, you have guessed it, with each breath he took in our Mr Duncan McTreggle began to rise steady-like, higher and higher with each intake of air. Whereas, if he had remained calm and breathed in and out normally, he would have stayed in his nice warm and comfortable *bed*.

But as it was, he held his breath and floated higher and higher, and moved closer and closer to the human's wrinkly and whiskery face, which was not what the little gnelf wanted to do at all.

…old is just another way of being young…

Ben Old whispered as he watched with amazement, "Now, my good gnome gentleman, don't you be getting uppity, I'm not a meanin' to be botherin' or upsetting you."

This *got to* Duncan a wee bit. "Bother me!" he squeakily shouted his thoughts. "But you've just made me and my wife wake up from a good sleep, and by, we are not gnomes, we are gnelfs!" Duncan paused for a flick of time or two, watching the human's expression, which did not change as the little gnelf let out some of his breath and began to sink back down to his grassy bed.

120

The woodsman could not help but feel a bit strange like, it was so weird. Here he was, at 80-odd years of age, seeing something that all his life he had always believed could happen but never been able to see or prove, until now.

He smiled down at the two little folks and continued to *talk* to them, "I wished my old ma and pa could see you two, they would have loved you to bits, and you would have made them so happy."

His smile widened as he whispered the words, his kindly manner helping the little gnelf lady to calm down a bit. Although it was still scary being so close to a human, she could somehow sense that it would be alright to be with the old human—he didn't look as if he would do them harm.

She breathed in slowly, keeping a tight handhold on the grass beneath her as she did so, and spoke to the old man as Duncan settled down with her, "Can we do anything for you, old human?"

It was all she could think to say.

The old human settled his wrinkly and whiskery face down a bit lower; to where Duncan and Isabella sat side by side, and keeping his whispering even quieter than before, he answered Isabella's question, "Yes, my little dear, you can tell me your name if ye would be so kind."

Isabella knew what *you* was, but she was not all that sure of who *ye* was; a problem that made her think that the humans are real odd-bod. Nevertheless, she told the old human just the same, "My name is Mrs Isabella McTreggle."

Funny, how it made her feel a bit proud when she said that. "And this is my husband, Mr Duncan McTreggle."

Talking to a human did feel a bit weird and wonderful somehow, but at the same time with this old man, it was as if it was the natural thing to do, but it did make her mutter to herself, "What was life going to chuck at me next, a talking tree that makes dinnertime meals?"

The old woodsman whispered as gently as he could, "I am happy to make your acquaintance, my dear. My name is Ben, *Old Ben* they call me here about."

It was obvious to Isabella why they called him Old Ben; he was old, wrinkly and whiskery old, wrinklier and whiskerier old than some of the old Elder Gnomes and Elder Elfs she had known in Blackwaterfoot Forest on the Isle of Arran, but not quite as whiskery as her husband.

Mr Duncan McTreggle suddenly got the idea; he being *The Elder* as it were, that it was time for him to speak, "This is getting us nowhere!"

"Please, Duncan! I'm talking to our new friend Ben Old, do you mind!"

The *do you mind* was not a question. Mrs Isabella McTreggle had worked things out in her clever mind and needed to put things in order. The new friend of theirs could prove to be useful, very helpful to them in their quest to find their new home world, and not to waste any more time.

"Right! My good new friend, Ben Old, we need your help. Can you tell us how to find a new home for ourselves?" *(Nothing like coming right to the point)*

With the fact that his wife had become *The Elder*, Duncan breathed out a long sigh of relief, and sank back just that bit further onto the soft bed of grass and weeds; to await things that might or might not happen, in comfort.

Meanwhile, the old woodsman was on the point of correcting Isabella's use of his name the wrong way round.

But then he thought, *Why? It didna matter that much*, and he answered the little lady's question, "Why, my little dear, I live in Bluewater Wood. Well, just a bit to the side of it you might say, an' I've been around here all my life, my dear, and I am sure it would make a real good home world for you."

Isabella was chuffed to bits. This was looking good. "Well, Ben Old, can you show us how to get there? Please!"

She had sensed a weird feeling when she had said *please*; it is a word that elves and gnomes, or gnelfs, seldom used, they never seemed to have the need of it; if you wanted something you wanted it and saying please only complicated things. Then, never mind, it did seem to make the old man smile.

Ben tried to stand up, his aching back was beginning to stiffen up even more than usual, and the pain was *summat awful*. (*summat* means *something*.) "Just a minute, my dear, I must ease my old back a wee while."

Isabella did understand Ben Old's problem; she'd met old gnomes and elves with *dodgy* backs in her younger days. But even so, she felt it only right and proper that she put the old man right on a certain matter that had little to do with backs.

Realising that the old man's head was moving up and away from her, Isabella thought she better shout, "Now, Ben Old, my name is Isabella McTreggle, and not *my little deer*!"

Ben Old lowered his head slightly, and Isabella continued in her more normal voice, "A *little deer* is an animal that lives in the glens and forests and on the hills, and I am not one of them. So, will you call me Isabella?" *(No* please *this time.)*

"Sorry, my…Sorry, Isabella, I didna mean to offend."

The old woodsman's apology was accepted, but he did not bring up the subject of him being called *Ben Old*, and he decided to leave it. Some other time, perhaps. He could sense that his new friend was getting a wee bit restless, and with a nod being as good as a wink to Ben Old, he straightened himself up by pushing his hands into the middle of his back.

By raising his voice just a bit, he tried to put matters in good order, "Right then, Isabella, even though you are in the wood already, Bluewater Wood it is. Wake your husband up and we will get on our way."

Ben Old reckoned that it would probably take them until suppertime to get to the wood proper; even though it was less than 10 minutes away if he were walking it himself. But these wee folk would not move as *fast* as he could. By the time they got to what he thought would be a good home place for them, daylight would be gone and he and his two *little* friends would be out in the dark.

Ben did not know at the time that gnomes, elves and gnelfs are okay to go about in the night dark if they so wish.

The other problem with night dark time on the Isle of Leodhais was that it could be cool, or even cold for that matter. And with this in mind, Ben Old, who did not like cool or cold much, thought he might rush off home, collect a warm jacket and come back for Duncan and Isabella. But would they wait for him? Would they trust him to come back for them?

There was only one way to find out, and it could mean that he would never see them again, but sometimes you just have to take the chance. "Right! Before I can take you to Bluewater Wood proper, I must go home and get me jacket to keep me warm when the night cold comes. Will you wait for me here? I'll be as quick as I can."

Duncan grabbed the chance to be *The Elder* again; he had to make a decision. "We can wait for you if you promise to return for us, and promise that you will see us safely to Bluewater Wood when you get back."

The old woodsman warmed to the little chap. "Don't you go a worryin' about any o' that, my little mate Duncan, I'll be back, don't you worry."

It was strange how the old woodsman; a man who had lived on his own for most of his adult life, could become a trusted companion to the new gnelfs after just one meeting. It was as if the three of them had known each other for a long time, which I suppose they had in a funny sort of way.

But more than likely it was the fact that Ben had lived along with Mother Nature all his life, and talking to little creatures was a natural thing for him to do.

When Ben Old had gone, the two gnelfs discussed matters, or rather Isabella talked while Duncan listened, even though Duncan was *The Elder*, with him being the oldest.

Isabella began to *discuss*. "He better come back…Or I'll put a wicked spell on him." *(She was good at laying down the law, so to speak, but she was apt to forget small details.)*

Duncan pointed out a small detail, "Come off it, Izzy, gnomes and elves, or gnelfs, don't do spells…Do they?!"

He had broken his *The Elder* silence in order to point out to his wife her lack of attention to detail.

Isabella reacted, "Yes! Well, *he* wouldn't know that, would he?" She was determined to be right.

Duncan had another go. "He wouldn't know about it anyway, he's not here now, is he?"

Isabella reacted again, "Duncan McTreggle! You are never satisfied unless you are making me out to be silly…Go and get another ache-head, will you, and leave me alone…I do not feel well, with all the nuisance! It's your fault anyway."

Duncan tried again, "But I was only—"

Isabella reacted yet again, speaking with her eyes closed, "*Only!* You call frightening me to death with noisy glary-eyed wrinkly whiskery monsters, making me follow smelly, old smelly goats. Then, leaving me on tops of tall trees, making me fall through thorns and prickles as big as, as big as…*Only!* Duncan McTreggle, you are, you're…You are a pee-wit-brain, yes, that's what you are, a pee-wit-brain."

Interruption over, Isabella opened her eyes and looked around for her husband, but it seemed that he had suddenly learned when to quit. Then, she managed to spot his green-kilted rear sticking out from a friendly leafy bush.

She gasped a wee bit. *Had she overdone it? Had she really given him an ache-head?*

Poor thing, he had only been trying to help her in his own pee-wit-brained sort of way.

But then, he shouldn't upset her the way he does though. *Serve him right, let him suffer*. The thoughts swirled around in her head.

Then, taking care how she breathed in, she took a breath to shout at the kilted rear of her husband, "Heh! Pee-wit! Are you alright?"

Mrs McTreggle should not have worried, *old pee-wit* was fine, and he was grinning from ear to ear inside his friendly leafy bush.

After a few chuckles settling flicks of time; safe in his bush, Duncan didn't want Isabella to know that he found the situation funny. And he left the green leaf sheltering smell of his bush and returned to the arms of his loved one, with just a slight sort of smile on his face.

But then one of the arms he was going back to, had a clenched fist on the end of it; one that his dear wife used to punch him, right in the middle of the soft puffing part of his tummy.

"Phooooo—"

Duncan's smile left his face as the wind left his stomach, and as he heard Isabella state that she did not like chuckling in secret. *(How did she know?)*

"That'll teach you not to make fun of me, you...Come here!" Her thoughts were mixed up, and she could not concentrate while she was wondering if Ben Old would come back and help them.

Within two flicks of time after Isabella had sunk her fisty hand into the whoopee-cushion of a tummy, her husband had settled himself to the discomfort of it, and she was doing her best to comfort him and help him to stand up straight, while seemingly ignoring the fact that he was finding it difficult to breathe.

She was sure in the knowledge that his face would eventually change from bright red to his more normal brown colour in a few flicks of time. To her, it was just a matter of waiting, but she did listen politely, and with a smile, to her husband's question.

"Wha...What you...Whaoof ...What you do that...Phaoof...What you do that for?"

Gradually, and very carefully, Duncan huffed and puffed his way to a more upright standing position, taking the hand that had a fist just a few flicks of time earlier had punched him into the dizzy world of *what the*!

Little by little, by controlled squeezing of his tummy and sides, and helped by his darling wife, Duncan regained something like his normal way of being. Then, by gently moving his mouth in a fish-like way and making the soft ghostly sound of *perwhop-whop* as he did so, he managed to regain the ability to perform the recognisable speech.

However, Isabella made her thoughts known before her husband could use the newly regained ability.

"I'm so sorry, Dunky, I couldn't help it…I'm a little bit bothered about Ben Old. *(Do not be around when she is a lot bothered Duncan.)* We've only just met him, and it doesn't seem right that we should trust him like we are doing, now does it?"

With mixed feelings in his thoughts and in his tummy, Duncan was finding it hard to be sure of anything. Even so, and despite the fact Isabella's bothering was much like his own, he tried to calm her and assure her that all would be fine and dandy. He had become *The Elder* again.

"You must not worry like that, Izzy, gnelfs don't worry, it hurts." Duncan thought to congratulate himself on making such a level-headed sentence, considering that he had only just got his proper breathing back. He continued. "I don't think Ben Old will let us down, Izzy, he's too old for that sort of thing. So, don't you fret yourself, just sit down here with me and watch the tiny creatures going about and doing what they do."

Author's Note:

Gnomes, elves, and gnelfs will often just sit and watch beetles and things for long periods of time.

So, they sat together, leaning back against a lump in the ground, a lump made of earth that some small creature had dug up, either in a search for food or to make a home. But if that creature had been successful, we will never know, but the earthy mound it had left behind was now serving the two gnelfs nicely and had a comfortable backrest. That is, if, the snoring from the two of them was anything to go by. They were asleep it would seem.

Ben Old walked up the grassy path to his cottage by the wood, on his old legs that had become sprightlier, a path he must have walked thousands of times in his long life. But this time it was different. His feet seemed to want to dance as he walked, and his knees and back did not seem to ache as they normally did.

Yes, it was unlike anything he had experienced before, in fact, his whole attitude seemed to be different. He had just met two little gnomes; or were it *gnelfs*? How more *different* could it get?

The old woodsman laughed aloud, laughed and laughed and laughed, until; it seemed, the natural world around him laughed along with him. He had never been happier, or if he had, it had been a long time ago when he was a young boy.

He knew in his heart that he could have told Duncan and Isabella how to get to Bluewater Wood; they were nearly there. It was only a few bends of the stream away from where they sat. But he wanted to be with them, to help them along, and as this thought passed through his mind his feet nearly did begin to dance, and if it hadn't been for the fact that his boot toes snagged in the long grass by the path, they probably would have.

However, all he could manage to do was to keep his balance by tottering along for a few steps and then satisfy his need to dance by tapping his hands against his thighs as he walked.

The fact that Ben had accepted his newfound friends said a lot about his trust in nature. He had been in Bluewater Glen and around Bluewater Wood for 80 years. And for every day of that long time, he had always accepted whatever Mother Nature sent his way and happily; that now, included two fairy folk called gnelfs.

A h-uile là chì 's nach fhaic!

uh hooluh lah ch-yee snach echk!

To all the future days!

Chapter 20
A Magic Moment for Ben Old

Light-day was going; fading away, and the birds were beginning to settle down for a rest in the night dark. Even the beetles and things were stopping what they were on with, and Mrs Isabella McTreggle was beginning to worry again, as she turned to look this way and that.

"I told you, didn't I? I told you we should not have trusted him. I told you—"

Then she was stopped in mid-sentence by a softly whispering voice, "Ben Old had returned."

"Hello, my Dears…Hello, Mr and Mrs McTreggle. I'm sorry, it took me a wee bit of a while. But if you're ready, we can get on our way now."

The one called Isabella was ready, but the one called Duncan was not. That gnelf was snoring, quite happy to wait for as long as it took Ben Old to come back.

Trying as hard as she could, Isabella could not seem to wake her snoring husband, and she looked up at Ben Old, shrugged her shoulders and raised her hands, and they waited.

The old woodsman struggled to sit down on the slowly dampening grass and weeds—the dew of dark night was beginning to form, and it was already wetting all the greenery around.

Author's Note:

But to say that Ben Old sat down is, perhaps, stretching the truth a wee bit, when, to be honest, it was really that he sort of collapsed in a heap, it was only the fact that he managed to land *in a sitting position that it could be said that he sat down. Anyway, he did.*

The old woodsman leaned to one side and looked down at the two little gnelfs, and even though it was getting darker, he could see they were, in fact, tired and weary. Especially, the one that had just stopped snoring and was rubbing his eyes as he sat up.

Keeping his voice down to a low whisper, Ben tried to nudge them into getting a move on, "Come on, my little…My little friends, don't you be a botherin', old…Ben Old will look after you. Come on now, it's not too far."

Isabella piffled and puffled a bit as she shook her yawning husband again, and more than once. Then, the little chap responded, "Whaa…sup? Go away!"

However, Mrs McTreggle wasn't about to go away, not without snoring-yawning Duncan McTreggle, even though it would seem that he'd gone back to sleep sitting up.

"Come on, Dunky! Ben Old is here. He's going to take us to our new home world."

Then, after one last shake of her husband's shoulder, followed by a thump in his side with the heel of her hand, and as if by magic, the snoring, snoozing and muffling noises stopped, and with one eye fully aware of the situation, with the other one still shut, Duncan McTreggle was awake. If only half so.

Ben Old smiled to himself, the back of his hand over his mouth, as he watched the waking-up antics of the two gnelfs, mumbling their names to himself while he watched Isabella coaxing her sleepy little husband into action.

The old man knew in his heart that he had found two new good friends; even though they were small friends, two that would, he was sure, make his old years happier. In truth, it made him feel cheery and content just by being there with them.

Keeping his voice in the low whisper he had found best to use, Ben spoke to Isabella, "It's alright, Isabella, don't you go a botherin' him too much. We've got plenty of time for us to…Even if it is getting dark, it isna so far as we need to worry ourselves. Take your time now, go easy." He saw the gnelf lady relax a wee bit, and he could sense the pressure of the need to hurry to get away from her.

The old woodsman continued, "There, you see, it doesn't do no good for young gnelfs to be a frettin' and a worryin', it isn't natural."

At the kind words spoken by the old woodsman, Isabella stroked her husband's face with her soft hand. She then turned to look up at Ben Old, and, with her face showing a kind of happy grace, she said something to him that he would never forget, "Ben Old, my old friend, you make my little heart smile, so just you rest yourself and take *your* time."

She spoke the words in her soft tinkling way; the way she talked when she was relaxed and happy.

Although he did not know why, the old man of the wood was changed by the lady gnelf's tinkling voice. He could feel himself becoming comfortably warmer somehow, and it seemed as if the last little bits of aches and pains in his old joints were melting away. He did feel wonderful—it was like being 20 again, *(well all right, 50ish then).* But he did feel a lot fitter and in good health.

Reaching out with the little finger of his rough right hand to stroke Isabella's hair in a gesture of thanks, he stopped himself.

Isabella stayed perfectly still, watching Ben Old as he tried to touch her hair. But when he stopped before his hand reached her, she took hold of his little finger in her two hands, pulled it down towards her, and kissed it.

That little show of affection between the old woodsman and the lady gnelf sealed their friendship—friends for life, and it was a real magical moment for Ben Old, as his old eyes watered a wee bit.

Author's Note:

Gnelfs do not know fear, and they do not cry. They never have a need to, they are too busy enjoying life. Even so, they love to be daring as they try to discover new things.

Chapter 21
Clarry

Making their way along the path was not very easy at first, as they tried to stay behind the old woodsman. In fact, it was uppity awkward, even with Ben Old trying not to stride his booted feet too far. While his new little friends did their best to keep up with him.

The two gnelfs float-walked here and there, scuffling through the grass and weeds at odd places while dodging the backward lashing nettles, and low gangly bramble branches that seemed to let Ben Old through; only to then shoot back at a fast rate towards the float-walking pair when the old woodsman's legs had gone by.

...gently read and quietly listen...

After getting away from a nasty-looking whip-lashing bramble branch just in time, Duncan shouted squeakily up to Ben Old's back and trouser-clad legs, "Heh! Ben Old! We canna be doin' this!" The gnelf had picked up the old woodsman's way of talking. "We've nearly been hurt with them yon bramble-bandits a whippin' back at us, can you not do somethin' about them?"

Hearing Duncan's high-pitched shout and feeling a bit guilty and a wee bit silly, Ben Old realised that he should have known how the brambles and things would behave.

The old woodsman stopped and turned to speak to his little friend. "Sorry, Duncan, I should have known better. I will be a lot more careful of them there bramble an' things from now on...Come on, 'tis not far now."

Isabella could not help but feel proud of and admire, her husband's show of strength of character in telling Ben Old about *them there brambles.* But it would have been better if he had talked to her first before he made the decision to be

The Elder. As they resumed their journey, she felt the need to bring something to her husband's attention.

"Dunky?" she was into the question thing again. "Why didn't you ask me about it?" her second question.

"What about, my dear?" Duncan was replying with a question of his own.

He did know *what* she was talking of, he just sort of let himself drift into the question way of things for the fun of it as the journey to their new world home continued.

Isabella's reply came after a slight pause as they followed Ben Old along the path, with her husband half turning to pay attention to his wife behind him, to listen carefully as she spoke.

"You should know what 'what' is and what it's about, shouldn't you? And you know I am not a deer!"

Ben Old was keeping out of it, although he did have a question of his own, a question he thought to himself, *What are they like?*

I think he meant that the two of them were just wasting time arguing in their squeaky way of talking.

Duncan looked up at Ben Old and seemed to know what the old man of the wood was thinking.

Then, as if to indicate the fact, the gnelf gentleman stopped, turned to his wife, and said, "Now then, Issy, we've no need to be like this. All I can say is, I am sorry. I should have spoken to you first, my Beloved, I see that now, but I had my gander up." *(Not very pleased about things.)*

Isabella seemed to be calming down a bit, and then a flash of something or other must have crossed her mind in a *hot* way.

"Gander up? What's *gander up,* when it is at home? I might add…Come on, Duncan McTreggle! Come on! What's *gander up* then?"

This time Ben Old poked his nose in as it were, and he bent down to look at the pair of them up close. He had enough of the bickering and arguing that had been going on. It seemed to the old woodsman that the two gnelfs were getting into time wasting with words just for the sake of it.

He spoke to them in a stronger way, but he still managed to keep his voice down to an easy listening whisper sort of level; in a kind fashion that they could not fail to hear with some sense of common sense.

"Now then, you two, let us not be a wastin' any more words and any more time, eh? Let us be gettin' on, we can sort out all of them; there questioning words when we get to where we are goin'…When we get to Bluewater Wood, eh? Can't we?"

The two gnelfs understood that the old man of the wood meant it to be as he said and that his last question was the last question, and credit to the two of them, they did not bother arguing with the old woodsmen, or between themselves. They just shrugged their tiny shoulders, took a couple of gulps of air, lifted off the path, and followed Ben Old like two little lambs.

Mind you, one of the *little lambs* was *piffling* and *paffling* quietly to herself as she float-walked behind the old woodsman with her husband.

It was night dark proper when the three of them entered the real part of Bluewater Wood at the gateway near Ben Old's cottage. The time was around the middle of the night dark, and after taking a few strides under the trees the old woodsman stopped, to bend down to speak with his new friends.

Author's Note:

I know you may be thinking why did Ben Old go back to his cottage for his jacket, and then, return to Duncan and Isabella, and then, take them to his cottage? I thought it odd myself but when I asked my little gnelf friend about it he just shrugged his shoulders, and we left it at that.

Ben had enjoyed walking along with the two gnelfs, even though they had argued a bit, but the strangest thing was that it seemed as though they had sort of floated along at times. But he couldn't be sure about it, being that they had been travelling behind him, and in the dark of late evening.

But there were a couple of other things that bothered the old woodsman; with the first one being:

'Would the two little gnelfs be safe in the dark wood?'

It was a strange new world to them, full of dangers, ones they might not know about, and the other thing was:

'Would he see them again if he left them, or they left him?'

Not questions really, more like *wonderings;* a word he sometimes used to describe his *thought-thinking*. All the same, he had to find out.

"Right, my little friends, if you will be kind enough to excuse me, I am off to me bed. It is way past my sleepin' time, so if you will be alright I'll be leavin' you." He paused for a moment or two and looked at the two little gnelfs. They just waved up at him and said something he couldn't quite make out, and then the two little figures walked slowly away from him; or were they *floating*?

...nice and easy is it...

It was too dark for the old woodsman to see the expressions on the faces of his two little gnelf friends, but he smiled as he imagined that they too would be smiling as they moved off into the dark of their new world home of Bluewater Wood.

Still, the old woodsman did not feel right about it, he was not comfortable with the thought of leaving the two of them to fend for themselves in a strange new world, especially in the dark.

He shouted after them, hoping that although he could not see them they would hear him just the same, "Duncan! Isabella! Now look here, it does not feel right that I will be leavin' you to…Leavin' you here in the woods, when you are more than welcome to come and stay with me in my cottage. It'll be nice and warm for you, and I'll be makin' some honey porridge if you would be wantin' some."

At a spot, just out of Ben Old's sight, a little way into Bluewater Wood, Duncan took it upon himself to be *The Elder* again and squeakily shouted back to the old woodsman, "It's fine, Ben Old, nice and fine…We will be fine, we are used to being out in the night dark. We like it for best." *(Oh dear!)*

Yes, he had done it again! He had forgotten the golden rule, the one that meant he should talk to his wife before becoming *The Elder* and making a decision.

"Duncan McTreggle! Why is it you never remember that you are my husband—my partner even? Why is it I am never asked? Eh?" *(Three questions in one breath.)*

Duncan replied, "But you didn't let me finish my…my loved one. I was going to ask you if you would like to stay in Ben Old's cottage, or would you be better if we were to find our new home."

Author's Note:
   What a creep. He had not meant to do that at all, he had just plain forgotten.

...we will see...

"Well! Ask me then!" Isabella had her suspicions.

"I have asked you!" Duncan was sticking it out to the end.

Isabella did her own version of sticking it out. "You just told me that you were *going* to ask me!" She was more suspicious now.

However, just at that moment, Isabella sensed that the way ahead would be a bit rough, and she allowed her husband to carry on, which he did, "I'm sorry, Izzy, I must be getting sleepy." He paused for a flick or two of time.

...gently and easy as you go...

Author's Note:

He is getting good at it, isn't he?

Taking things seriously, he asked a question, "Would you like, us to stay in Ben Old's cottage then?"

There followed a long pause, during which the both of them could hear the sounds of the woodland: the swish of a night bird's wings, the rustling of leaves, with the lighter rustling of grass as a rabbit moved along one of the rabbit paths under the bushes, and they could smell the stinky aroma of a fox.

Then, as they heard the hoot of an owl not far off, Isabella answered her tired husband's question, "Yes, Dunky, yes, that would be nice for us. I think we should go back to Ben Old and his warm cottage."

She could feel herself tingling at the way her husband had been a bit *do-gooding*, but she allowed him that they were both tired, and she took his hand as the owl hooted a last farewell; while they wondered what a *cottage* was, as they made their way along the path, floating along easily.

The old woodsman had been waiting at the gate at the side of the wood, unsure of what the two gnelfs were doing; or where they had got to. Then, he saw them coming towards him in the dim darkness of the path they had used to enter the wood, and he was happy that they were coming back to him.

With a sigh of relief, which soon turned into a big yawn, the old woodsman asked his new friends to come and get their heads down for the night in the safe warmth of his cottage.

Ben Old's cottage had been standing at the side of Bluewater Wood for hundreds of years. Its thick stone walls had held up against many cold Scottish winters, with the inside being kept nice and warm by the simple method of having an open fire always giving out its heat from the hearth all winter long. It was as if the fire's heat had *soaked* its way into the stone of the walls, all around the building.

Even though it was springtime and a warm springtime at that, the old woodsman and his two little companions were pleased to feel the warmth of the cottage as they stood in the small kitchen/living room, with the gentle sensation becoming even cosier when Ben Old closed the heavy wooden door of the cottage. However, there was one other creature enjoying the warmth of the little cottage by the wood.

It was Clarry the Cat. She was the other creature that Ben Old kindly made known to the two gnelfs, his new friends.

The old woodsman could see that his new friends were a wee bit uncomfortable and spoke softly to the two of them, "Now, you two, you are not to worry about Clarry, she's an old tabby cat who will do you no harm. She'll just sniff around you, sort of have a look-see at you, and then, she will leave you alone."

Duncan and Isabella had been watching Clarry making ready to have her *look-see* with the cat stretching herself by digging the long sharp claws of her front paws into the soft rug by the hearth and pushing her back up in a tall curve; showing how sure she was of her position in the household. But Clarry the Cat wasn't ready for what followed.

"Hello, Clarry, my name is Duncan McTreggle, and this is my wife Isabella. Hope you don't mind, but we've been asked to sleep here, to wait for light-day morning."

Clarry could have rolled over on her back and kicked her legs up in the air with joy, at last, someone or something, that could actually speak her language. She had met other little folk in the wood before, but they had never said a word, and it had been Clarry talking to Clarry for years and years, 'til now, and while all she had understood of Ben Old was that he made odd sort of noises, just as he was doing then.

"Now, come on, Clarry, be nice. They are our guests. Don't you start getting pernickety now."

"What's the old fellow on about? I've never understood a word he says!" Clarry loved it, loved the way she had just asked a question. She then asked another, "What are your names again?"

136

"My name is Duncan, and this is my wife Isabella." *Duncan was being The Elder again.*

Clarry purred loudly as she acknowledged the little creature's reply, "Yes, that's it, Duncan."

It was absolutely great, talking to the little creature, so she asked another question, "And what are you?"

"We are gnelfs!"

Clarry spoke a contented confirmation, "Yes, that's it—gnelfs."

Oh, joy of joys, it really did feel out of this world, asking someone a question, (*yes a gnelf must be a someone and not a something*) and, hopefully, one Clarry was about to get an answer to, and one she could understand.

Duncan answered Clarry politely, "Oh, Ben Old is just being his old self, just wanting to be a good friend." He looked at Isabella as he spoke, and was happy and relieved to see her smiling. This, in his book, meant it was all right for him to carry on being *The Elder*, for the time being at any rate.

Ben Old was just a mite confused. Was the cat talking *gnelf*, or was the gnelf talking *cat*? He would leave it 'til morning.

Isabella had not felt so cosy in a long while, she was smiling at her husband and Clarry.

Then as the old woodsman wished them all a goodnight, the little gnelf lady said her goodnight in a soft tinkly voice, "We'll be just fine, Ben Old, we will be just fine. See you in light-day beginning, eh?"

With the fire in the hearth flickering yellow and orange, they all made their own preparations for a settled and warm dark-time sleep, and within a few flicks of silent time that followed the preparations, the cottage was quiet—warm, snug, and quiet.

In the bedroom upstairs, Ben Old took a bit longer than usual to settle once he'd got down under his blanket; with his thoughts dwelling on the special evening he'd had—an unbelievably special kind of evening and half a night. He knew that if anyone had told him about it, he wouldn't have believed them.

Then, as he lay there wondering, Isabella's *tinkly* voice came back to him in his thoughts, and…he…nodded…off…to…sleep as the smoke drifted up out of the cottage chimney in the cool of the night dark air.

Author's Note:

Gnelfs are usually only seen by humans who can accept the truth of a fairy world, but when gnelfs are there, more often than not, they will just be something spotted for a fleeting moment, out of the corner of the eye as it were. Be ready.

Chapter 22
Another Way with Fish

Things in the dark of night dark time usually look different to what they do in light-day time, and it was just so in Bluewater Wood.

While those in the cottage slept their warm sleep, the many creatures who found Bluewater Wood to be a good place to be living in, even at dark nights, went about finding good supplies of food in the mist and dewy damp of the woodland.

The creatures of the night dark used every part of the wood, all the way down the south side of Bluewater Glen, through the trees by the side of Ben Old's cottage, and to the stream at the bottom of the glen, with a few more trees by the other side of the trickling clear water.

The only parts of the wood that could be seen from the outside at night dark were the tallest of the tall trees with their full shadowy black shapes totally different from the dressings of fluttering green leaves that would be seen in the new light-day.

Bluewater Wood at night dark was the same wood of light-day, but it was *different*. It was quieter; it was spookier, in fact, not a nice place to be unless you were a night dark creature. And the four *creatures* asleep in Ben Old's cottage were quite happy not to be night dark creatures, for that one night, at least.

The beginning of light-day had been around for a good many flicks of time before Clarry tested the air with her whiskers and nose, and then, suggested they go and see if Ben Old needed reminding that night dark had finished.

…Yes, cats do talk…

Isabella answered the whiskery cat sleepily, "Aw…iss…a'right if you go, Clarry. We will just stay here for a bit longer. We are still a bit…a bit tired."

The lady gnelf had spoken without opening her eyes, in fact, she hardly opened her mouth, but Clarry understood what had been said; that gnelfs were lazy, or so it would seem.

Yes, alright…First morning and all that, just this once mind, Clarry let the kind thought run through her head as she stretched herself down from the comfortable and warm armchair by the fire.

Then, purring in her *early-morning-before-food* way, she assured the sleepy gnelf lady on the warm hearthrug, "That's alright, you two wake up nice and slow. I'll go and see if—"

Clarry stopped talking to look up at Ben Old, who had just appeared at the doorway at the bottom of the stairs.

Wish he would not creep about so, thought Clarry as she stopped halfway through another stretch, and then jumped back onto the armchair, to purr in a grumbling-angry sort of way.

"None of that, Clarry. If I'm up, you're up," Ben Old had said that for more mornings than he could remember or count, and always with the same result, Clarry would curl up and close her eyes.

Duncan struggled to sit up. It was so cosy by the fire, and even though it had quietened down to just a few glowing embers, the steady warmth had softened him through the night dark, and his body was in need of a good stretch.

"Duncan! Do you mind? I'm trying to sleep," Isabella thought it proper to point out to her stretching husband that elbows can be hard, and pointy when shoved into the back of a tired gnelf, especially, lady gnelfs who were still half asleep and intending to stay that way.

Ben Old turned away from what he thought should be a private talk between a little husband and wife and went to attend to his morning duties in the kitchen part of the room.

…And gnelfs can listen…

Meanwhile, Clarry sat up to lick at her paws in order to wash behind her ears, only to then change her mind and smoothly drop down from her chair to walk silently over to Ben Old; to wait by his feet for her morning drink of water, with her tummy ready for the first meal of the day…Fish!

As soon as the lid of the tin of cat food had been removed, there was an almighty disturbance on the hearthrug.

Duncan sat up on one elbow, curious as to what Clarry was having for breakfast—it seemed to have the smell of fish, while his wife lay on her side with her eyes focused on the old man and his cat.

"Duncan! Duncan! Duncan! Oh dear, oh my goodness, oh…I canna believe it. Oh, my life!" Isabella's hand slowly closed over her mouth as she turned to look away from the scene at the kitchen end of the room, with her eyes firmly shut.

That animal, that *creature*, was eating another animal…It was disgusting.

Isabella had realised that Clarry was eating a fish, and the lady gnelf's body had gone cold as she sat up with a sudden jolt, a sudden move that had the unfortunate result of her head hitting her bleary-eyed slowly rising husband with a good smack under his chin, and, as knockout blows go, it was a cracker.

A low sleepy kind of moan escaped through Duncan's open mouth, with his yawn stopping halfway, and he dropped down onto the rug beneath him, into the dreamless sleep of a knockout. The little gnelf was *out for the count* as they say.

Isabella ignored the slight ache-head she seemed to have found, and stirred herself with the sickly thought of what Clarry was doing, while at the same time, she chose to ignore her husband's sudden drop onto the rug that was their bed.

Even though she had an ache-head that had sort of found its way to the middle of her forehead; just below the point where she had made hard contact with Duncan's chin, she managed to speak to Clarry-the-fish-eater, "Clarry Cat, you are more evil than I can say. How can you? How can you eat another animal? It is…It's—" Isabella stopped, her throbbing head had gained a mind-numbing ache that was just too much, and her hesitation gave Clarry the chance to defend her eating habit.

"But, my dear, the fish is dead, and it's all in bits, bite-sized bits. What can be wrong with that?"

Then, as if to show the tasty fairness of her breakfast, Clarry delicately placed one of her clean front paws in the dish of fish, (*say the last three words a bit quickly*) and began to lick every last bit off her fish-picking paw. (*And those!*)

Isabella turned white with horror. How could such a lovely soft furry tabby cat be so cruel, so evil and so unfeeling? It was more than she could stand.

"Duncan! Duncan, we are leaving…*Now!*" the words spoken with her clear gnelf-like way of speaking seemed to echo around the confines of the quiet kitchen/living room, while her tummy seemed to turn and bubble.

141

Isabella adjusted her clothes, pulled at her husband's sleeve, and glared at the offensive Clarry, all at the same time.

Author's Note:

Amazing. But had Duncan heard what she had said about their sudden unplanned departure?

Clarry sat up, purring softly, with her tail curled loosely round by her feet, and the tip of it flicking in a foot-tapping way. Then, as quick as it had started, her tail stopped its flicking, and her eyes narrowed a wee bit, with her whiskers trembling as Isabella came across the room.

As the gnelf lady approached, Clarry had something more to say, "Young lady, might I point out to you?"

Then, Isabella's face-to-face contact with the upright fish-eater had the effect of stopping anything that Clarry might have said in her defence. Then, there was the fact that Isabella didn't waste any time in having her say, "Don't you be *young ladying* me, you…you…you *feliney* cat, you!"

Duncan rubbed his eyes; he was amazed; not to mention not fully awake, and his weary sleep-emptied mind began to fill with a pattern of thoughts.

Feline? Where did she get that from? It sounded right… But was it right?

No matter, Isabella continued chastising Clarry, "Look here, you fish-eating evil feline cat. I have no doubt that you will have every excuse going as to why you eat other creatures. Maybe, it is not even your fault. Maybe you just canna help it, and it is how things are. But I still think it's disgusting."

She couldn't go on, it was too much, and Clarry, who could see that the little gnelf lady was tired and a mite upset, did her best to show that even though she was a feline cat, she did care about other creatures.

"Look, Isabella, I'm sorry. I didna mean to upset you, believe me…Please!"

Clarry lowered her head a wee bit more to sniff at Isabella's nose, trying to show in her cat-like way that she would prefer that they stay friends.

Isabella drew back slightly as she could smell dead fish on Clarry's breath, and a few flicks of time passed by as the two of them looked at each other in silence.

Then, they spoke together, "We'll work it out somehow."

The combination of Clarry's purring cat voice and Isabella's tinkly way of talking made Ben Old laugh. It was as if Clarry and Isabella were trying to sing with, of course, Duncan who was getting back up on one elbow again, following with a *musical*, "Of course, we will!"

Ben Old leaned back in his chair by the kitchen table, clamped his hands on his knees, and rocked with laughter as he listened to the two little folk and Clarry *singing*; he had not enjoyed himself so much in a long time.

It is, perhaps, fortunate that no other humans were within listening distance of Ben Old's cottage at that particular time. Fortunate in the sense that the mixed series of meowing sounds would have given the foursome in the cottage the problem of being discovered, which would have been slightly awkward, to say the least.

As it was, the existence of the two gnelfs remained a secret, and Clarry was forgiven. After all, she was what she was, and even Mother Nature could not change that.

But since that first breakfast together, Clarry has always been careful to eat her meals in private, and on the quiet so to speak, whenever gnelfs were present.

Even though Ben Old had been retired from his official duties of woodsman to the Sannox Estate for a good many years, he still made it his business to keep an eye on things, with the result that the paths, fences, stiles and gates were kept in reasonably good order.

Of course, the five-barred gate and the one-step stile near his cottage were treated regularly to his attention; he used them more than the other gates and stiles that were on the boundary of Bluewater Wood.

It had been the gate the old woodsman had helped the two gnelfs through in the night dark just gone by. And just as it had somehow *welcomed* Duncan and Isabella to Bluewater Wood in the dark, it seemed to welcome them with a mellower and softer feeling in the light-day beginning.

With its warm and weathered wood frame feeling comfortable in his hand, Ben Old swung the wooden gate open, allowing the two gnelfs to float-walk to Middle Trail through the open gateway with ease.

The old chap also stepped through, and let go of the gate. Then the three of them watched it swing slowly back to the closed position with a gentle but positive *bummmmp*.

Then, Ben Old looked down at his two little companions, his new friends. "Now then, my special friends, I would be happy to come with you and help you find your new home, but if you would prefer to take a look for yourselves, private like—" He lifted his hands palms upwards as he spoke. "Would you?"

He thought it best that he put it that way, they would more than likely be unsure about telling him to mind his own business, so, it would be better if he gave them an easy way to tell him.

"Well…If you dunna…If you don't mind!" Duncan spoke kindly to the old woodsman; an old man he had taken a strong liking to, even though he was a human.

As it was, the way that Duncan stated his and Isabella's desire to be on their own for a while made Ben Old easy in his mind, and the old woodsman and the two gnelfs were content to leave it at that.

Bidding the two new little people of Bluewater Wood farewell and not knowing if he would meet up with them again, Ben Old turned round to swing the big gate to its open position enough for him to step through to his cottage side of the gateway.

He then allowed it to swing back to its closed position, and with an easy movement that involved lifting his arms; so that they rested on the gate's top wooden bar, he stood there quietly and took in the early morning fragrance of warm dewy wood, with the mist moving around the trees before it would fade away.

He watched the two small green-clad gnelfs float-walk away, along a pathway/track into the middle of Bluewater Wood—to look for a new home, and he silently wished them all the luck in the world, their world and his. Then, taking one last look into the wood, the old woodsman walked slowly back to his cottage, and Clarry, his fish-eating cat.

Author's Note:

If you wish to meet with a gnelf, all you need do is start by just being kind to all and everything you meet.

I was told this by Duncan McTreggle, the Gnelf Elder of Bluewater Wood, that my kindness to all living things, and my belief in little folk, made it easy for him to meet and talk with me in the first place.

Chapter 23
In the New World of Bluewater Wood

The two gnelfs made their slow and easy way along the Middle Trail of Bluewater Wood for a while; the trail goes from one side of the wood to the other, and then they made a right turn to go down the wood by following the leafy *Bottom Trail*.

Duncan was overjoyed at being in their new world at last, and as he glanced around at the many different trees and bushes, and the woodland flowers in the shining reflection of the sunlight flickering through the leafy canopy of the trees, it made him feel that he just had to say something.

"Just look at it." Meaning the surrounding nature of their new world.

Then, he said something about something else; something he had spotted when his looking had wandered freely. "Izzy! Look at that! It's peefrect *(perfect)* for us, don't you think?"

The little gnelf had placed his hand on his wife's shoulder, and he had then *pointed her* in the right direction, in order that she could have the chance to see what he could see; a gigantic oak tree. The one he was sure would make a grand home-tree, their new home in the new world of Bluewater Wood.

They had just come out from under a *tunnel arch*, one made of the low-hanging branches of bushes that grew along Bottom Trail. There, right in front of them in a small clearing, was the oldest, tallest and widest oak tree they had ever seen. *Big Oak*. The tree was surrounded by the greenest carpet of short grass and the prettiest flowers they could ever wish for.

Big Oak's trunk and branches looked massive to the two gnelfs, with its position making it look as if it had grown on the top of a grass-covered mountain, with the ground sloping away from it in every direction. But in truth, it was the other way around.

It was the grass and flower-covered ground that had settled around the tree; having naturally spread over and around Big Oak's huge roots and trunk, with the odd root or two poking up above the grassy carpet in places, with their shiny bark skin looking as if it had been polished and cleaned by Mother Nature herself. Which, of course, they had.

All around Big Oak, under its outspreading branches, the grass was so short and soft, and so dense in growth, that it seemed to be laid out like a luxury carpet. Without a weed in sight, just pretty flowers of blue, yellow and white, or so it would seem.

Isabella was delighted with the thought of such a wonderful home, and in such a magnificently beautiful setting, and she just glowed inside, with her mind wandering over what she would be able to do with their new house.

However, before putting her thoughts into words, Isabella thought it best to let her husband sort of pick up the feelings she was giving out in his own good time, and then he could gradually agree with the alterations she wanted.

While Mrs Isabella McTreggle herself had already decided things, there could not be a better home in Bluewater Wood or Bluewater Glen or Blackwaterfoot Forest for that matter. However, Mr Duncan McTreggle had yet to come to terms with the fact that their search for a new home had ended.

Nevertheless, Mrs Isabella McTreggle was certain that Big Oak was going to be their new home in their new world, and without further ado, she began to climb up the side of their new address. Once she had decided on some course of action, Isabella would not be easily made to change her mind, and her new home was one she would never leave.

...Bluewater Wood is such a beautiful place to be...

Mr D. and Mrs I. McTreggle
Big Oak
Bluewater Wood
Bluewater Glen
Near Steornabhagh
The Isle of Leodhais
Alba

Isabella thought things through as she climbed, judging it would probably be best if she informed her husband of their new address after she had persuaded Ben Old to make them a few things—like a door!

But she would not have to explain to Duncan with regard to the address. The new Elder of Bluewater Wood had worked it out for himself. Then, not many flicks of time after he had found a large population of minnows in a slow-moving part of the stream just around the corner as it were, on the other side of some boggy marsh.

A h-uile là chì 's nach fhaic
uh hooluh lah ch-yee snach echk
To all our future days.

Chapter 24
The Woodens

Resisting the temptation to try out his minnow-tickling skills in Bluewater Wood, Duncan had contented himself by just being happy to inspect that part of the stream for future reference; moving carefully along the bank so as not to disturb the fish in their calm clear water of a home too much.

Then, satisfied that all would be well, come the day when he did venture out to try his minnow-tickling skills. Then, he returned to his wife to attend to her desires with regard to their new home.

But, being a dedicated minnow-tickler, Duncan did give the matter of minnow-tickling some further thought as he had float-walked his way back from his inspection of the stream. He bothered himself with the thought of how it might be a bit of a problem having to cross the boggy marshland to go minnow-tickling.

But then, he thought; by taking care of which route he might possibly follow, it could be that he could maybe float-walk for most of the way. While only stopping here and there to work out each following bit of the journey, he would hopefully, avoid the many pools of water of unknown depth that were scattered around.

He was aware that some of the pools were hiding behind tall clumps of spiky reeds and grass, and with one or two even hidden under *false* carpets of grass and moss as if waiting to trap the unwary float-walking gnelf.

...But there were more than pools of water hiding from his gaze...

Unbeknown to Duncan, two other little folk of Bluewater Wood were watching him; little folk who went by the title of Woodens, little folk who dressed in brown and lived above and below ground, and were Bluewater Wood natives.

Author's Note:

Gnelfs are tubby and dress mainly in green, and can float-walk. While Woodens are slim, slightly smaller than gnelfs, and dress in brown, and the fact that they had wings, did made it possible for them to fly.

While her husband was away on his minnow-tickling business, Isabella had done a bit of inspecting. She had checked Big Oak carefully, and in the course of her inspection, the First Lady Gnelf of Leodhais had found a nice *cave* of an old woodpecker's nest in the old tree.

The *cave* was at a spot where a thick branch in the second set of branches from the ground grew out from the tree's huge trunk, and just where Big Oak's trunk seemed to be nearly as wide as the kitchen/living room in Ben Old's cottage, and it did smell different.

It was 'peefrect', (perfect) all Duncan would have to do would be to make the cave *entrance bigger.*

The cave's last owner hadn't been so particular; not like the average lady gnelf that is. The lady gnelf in question had considered the entrance to her new home would have to be made slightly taller and a little wider, and, of course, also have a door fitted, Ben Old would make a door for them as soon as he knew they needed one.

The making of the McTreggle's new home begins.

With nothing more than the knife he carried in his belt, Duncan started work on the doorway to their new home. Isabella having squeezed herself through the woodpecker-sized entrance, began tidying, altering, cleaning, renovating and sweeping while muttering, "Piffle, paffle, piffle, piffle," and so on.

Author's Note:

Duncan's knife is no bigger than a sparrow's beak.

Some flicks of time later:

"I'm hungry!" Duncan made the appeal as he laid down his knife carefully; it was still sharp, even though he had been using it without stopping.

He leaned with one shoulder on the rough *skin* of Big Oak. He then poked his head through the doorway he had been working on, and repeated his statement a wee bit louder, "I tell you, I'm hungry!" he shouted the words into their new home, in the hope that Isabella would hear him; understand and feel sorry for him.

Perhaps, she might even agree with him that it was dinnertime, who knows? *He'd be lucky!*

The not-so-tinkly voice echoed from within. "Hungry? We haven't got time to be hungry. I want to get this home ready for when Ben Old brings the new door. So don't go on about wandering off to look for food—just grab a couple of oak leaves, Dunky! I'm sure Big Oak won't mind."

Duncan drew his head back, a wee bit mystified. "What new door?" He thought the question and mouthed it silently.

He may as well have shouted it! Mrs McTreggle answered her husband's thought just one flick of time after he had mouthed it, "He's going to make us a door to fit the entrance you are getting ready—"

The gnelf lady then paused for a flick or two of time and then asked the question that Duncan was sure would follow, "Have you finished it yet?"

Isabella had read his mind, and had known what he had been thinking, or could it be that she knew her husband only too well? *I wonder?*

Taking his knife from its resting place, Duncan flicked at a few bits of Bog Oak's bark skin and leaned in through the doorway again, to answer his wife confidently, "Yes, my dear, it's ready." Then he paused to flick a couple more bark-skin bits and then continued, "Is Ben Old? Does Ben Old *know* that he is making a new door for us, Isabella?"

Mrs McTreggle came to the entrance to her home, pushed her head out, ran her hands over the work her husband had done, and looked closely at the newly shaved section where he had made the doorway taller and wider. She was pleasantly surprised. But all the same, she didn't show it. She could see that he had done an excellent job of work, in fact, she could go so far as to say that her husband was a first-class wood-gnelf, but she didn't.

All she did say was, "I suppose you better go and tell…Go and *ask* Ben Old if he can come and make us a door and fit it for us."

Duncan wondered. *But that would mean that he would know where we lived!*

Author's Note:

Is what follows further proof that Isabella could read her husband's mind, and know what he was thinking?

"You are quick on the take up *(uptake)* aren't you, my dear husband, you should eat *more* oak leaves."

The fact that his wife was being sarcastic escaped Duncan, and he was pleased with himself. It was not all that often he was the receiver of praise from his dear wife, and Isabella could see that he had listened to her words for a change and that he had accepted what she had said as praise, as he thanked her.

"Why, thank you, Isabella."

Being of a kindly disposition, Isabella just let it go, he had not even bothered to ask her what *uptake* she thought he was good at.

There's only one Duncan, she thought and smiled with an easy love for her chubby husband.

Ben Old was pleased to help the two gnelfs when Duncan asked him about the new door, and straight away collected his tool bag, while pointing out to his little gnelf friend the certain bits of plank-wood they would probably need. Then, with plank-wood at the ready, they set off to go make and fit a new door in Big Oak before night dark came.

Ben Old was carrying a couple of planks in his hand by holding them to the handle of his tool bag, while Duncan did his best to half walk and half float-walk with two smaller bits of wood on his shoulders.

The extra weight of the bits of wood made the little gnelf take in bigger gulps of air, which meant that he dropped down to the ground more often than was normal for him. But, between them, they eventually got the plank-wood safely to Big Oak, where Isabella was waiting patiently, or so it would seem.

Seo àite fasgach
shaw ah-tchuh fasskoch
Here is a sheltered spot.

Chapter 25
Making a Good Choice

Ben Old could see why the two gnelfs had chosen Big Oak, and he thought it only right that he should tell them they had made a good choice. Then, whistling softly to himself, the old woodsman climbed up the tree a bit at a time and got to work on the new door, concentrating on making it so it would fit nice and snug in the opening made bigger by Duncan with his tiny knife.

Sure, that all was as it should be, and that he had done a really good job, the whistling woodsman covered the new door with some of Big Oak's bark skin, and then, handed the finished item to his friends Duncan and Isabella.

Bang, chop, scrape, knock, clatter, a bit of tiffle, taffle, tuffle, traffle, triffle, stuffle, staffle, and the new door was in place, with its bark skin hiding it from view, and just before time-tea meal.

Seeing that his wife had a sort of satisfied look about her as she admired the new door. Also, the fact that he didn't want to eat any more of Big Oak's leaves, Duncan took the plunge to be *The Elder*.

With his tummy begging him to do just that, he fairly *sang* the words. "Right! Shall we have our time-tea meal then?"

The hope in his *singing* voice did not go unnoticed.

"Dunky, my wonderful—" Even as she spoke, Isabella was thinking that maybe *wonderful* was going a bit over the top, so she rearranged things slightly.

"Duncan…My husband, I will prepare for us a magnificent time-tea meal, one that you will remember for—" She paused for a flick of time or two and then continued in a calm manner, "But we shall have to eat outside, we don't have a table, or chairs or benches inside our new home."

Ben Old's ears pricked up, and he just had to interrupt. He had the right thing or things in his workshop-shed at the back of his cottage. "It's no problem. You come along and have tea with Clarry and me, and after tea, I will show you some tables and chairs, and things that will be just right for your new home." He looked down at his little friends, and whispered, "What do you say?"

The old woodsman was eager to help where he could, and he looked at the two gnelfs hopefully.

Isabella answered in her tinkly voice, making the old man feel that he had just said the right thing, "Ben Old, my dear friend, that is very kind of you, and if it isn't too much trouble, and if it won't put you out, we will be glad to have a tea meal with you... Won't we, Duncan?"

Duncan said that he would be very willing to take a meal with the old woodsman and his cat, but he was wondering what Isabella had meant by *put you out*. He pondered on this for a while, then, he forgot all about it.

Satisfied that they had done a good job between them; and that the door was all finished and fitted, the three of them got ready to make their way to Ben Old's cottage; with the old woodsman climbing back down to the ground in just a few flicks of time.

Author's Note:

How can you put somebody out and have tea with them?

The woodsman might be old, but he could still climb and unclimb, and he made it look very easy as he shuffled himself along the branch he had been sitting on, with his feet touching the next branch down. He then lowered himself to sit on the branch his feet had been touching, and from there it was an easy matter to just slowly slide down to the ground.

While Ben Old had been making his slow and easy way back down to the grass-carpeted floor of that particular part of Bluewater Wood, Duncan and Isabella had clambered down the other side of Big Oak. The two gnelfs changed their small hands and feet from one hand or foothold to another in quick easy moves, it was as if they were small squigs going on the lookout for some food-nuts.

On the journey to Ben Old's cottage, Isabella busied herself collecting things for their tea meal, seeking out and picking goodies of all kinds—leaves, grasses, flowers, and seeds, not to mention the eatables under the ground, roots and things. It would seem that the time-tea meal was going to be a real good one, as the lady gnelf had said, and what is more, it was.

...

Ben Old's workshop-shed was big enough to keep a farmer's tractor in, which was what it had been used for in the past. There were big barn-type doors at either end, and windows in the roof and down each side, with a small door tucked in a corner on the side nearest to Ben Old's cottage, and it was this door that creaked open as the old woodsman escorted his two little friends into the building after they had eaten their tea meal.

Ben Old casually lifted his legs as he walked in through the side door, so as to clear the high entrance, while Duncan and Isabella struggled and climbed over the obstruction.

With a bit of "wuffle, wiffle, waffle, wattle, wottle," and so on as Isabella spoke her thoughts relating to workshop-shed steps.

But the two little gnelfs did make it through the doorway, to the inside of the big building, to be then truly amazed at the hundreds of different items of furniture, toys, tools, and more toys.

This miniature world also included what Ben Old called a *Doll's House*; a house that looked to be good enough, and big enough for Duncan and Isabella to live in; if they were so minded to do so that is. Oh well, maybe not. But it *was* big, in gnelf terms.

Ben Old could see that the two gnelfs were enjoying themselves, just as he was, and he only had to note their excited chatter to measure how much.

"Ooooh! Look here, Dunky, wouldn't it be nice!" Isabella had spotted a doll's chair, one that was just about her size.

"Aah! But just look at these, my dear!" Duncan easily attracted his wife's attention.

She was looking around after all, and he pointed out two rocking chairs that had been simply, but stoutly made from *twisted twigs*, and were of a size to suit Mr and Mrs McTreggle.

It would seem that all the toy furniture, and other things, had been made by Ben Old himself. And as he looked at, and listened to the two gnelfs, nothing would have pleased him more than for them to have what he had originally made, for no other reason than to obtain enjoyment and satisfaction from doing so.

He was a woodsman who loved being good with wood of all kinds, including twigs and thin soft willow, and seeing his new little friends loving his work gave the old man a good satisfying feeling, knowing that the things he had made were being admired and enjoyed, and would soon be put to good use.

Even though the twiggy rocking chairs weren't all that heavy, *(not in our terms that is)* and even though gnelfs are strong for their size, the weight of the chairs was enough to put a stop to Duncan and Isabella float-walking with them, no matter how many deep big breaths they took. What were they to do?

They did not want to walk with them all the way back to Big Oak, that would be silly. But what else could they do? They could ask Ben Old to carry them, a suggestion that was to Duncan's liking. On the other hand, they could ask to borrow the toy trolley-truck, with its pulling and steering handle and four soft bouncy wheels.

Duncan asked Ben Old about the trolley-truck, and the old woodsman was only too happy to let them have it. "Of course, you can borrow it, Duncan my old friend. Of course, you can, and any time you like."

The old woodsman was pleased as punch, to think that the smart looking trolley-truck with a red body and yellow wheels could be used for such a good purpose. He was sure it was why he had made it.

The words *any time you like* got the old man thinking, *Now, then, if they are going to borrow things and I'm not around?*

His hand rubbed at his whiskery chin for a few flicks of time before he spoke, then, with a wide smile on his face, he thought how good it would be to tell his friends his idea, and he did, without realising he was doing so.

"Ah yes! That's it, I'll mek 'em a little door and give 'em a key of their very own…Yes, that's what I'll do."

He had been talking to himself, putting his thoughts into words, without realising that his two friends were listening.

He was a wee bit surprised when Isabella asked, "What door? What key? Who?"

Author's Note:

Three questions in one breath. She was good at it.

Isabella's questioning had put Duncan on his guard and he thought, *Oh, here we go again—questioning time.*

However, Ben Old proved the little gnelf chap wrong as he spoke to Isabella, "Now, don't you go startin' on me with your questions, pretty lady. I'm just goin' to mek a door for you and Duncan, and I'm goin' to put a lock on it and give you a key, and that's that, no arguments."

He wagged a finger in the direction of Isabella, to show that he meant what he said.

Author's Note:

It was his use of pretty lady*, that saved the day as it were, and the old woodsman got away with it.*

Isabella had not been told that she was a pretty lady before, and she loved it, and she loved Ben Old for giving her the new title.

"Piffle, paffle, puff," Isabella began to show how displeased she was.

But the old woodsman stopped her and smiled as he spoke calmly but firmly to her, "An' you can pack that in. It's not nice for a pretty lady to curse, even if, it only pretends to curse. Now, let's have no more, Isabella, eh?"

But even with the trolley, and Ben Old's help, it wasn't going to be easy moving furniture and things for half the width and length of Bluewater Wood.

They used the Middle Trail from the cottage to the middle of the wood, and then Bottom Trail to Big Oak. But by being careful, and by choosing the right bits of furniture to move first, the McTreggles would be spending their first full night dark in Big Oak in a fairly comfortable way, thanks to Ben Old.

Big Oak was their new home, and Bluewater Wood was their new world. And Ben Old was their new dear friend.

Things were looking good for the one-time gnome and one-time elf, and it was not long in light days and night darks before the two of them were settled down snugly in their new home in Big Oak, with the door made by Ben Old making it warm and cosy by keeping out the night dark damp and mist.

But even with the door closed they could hear the sounds of the wood, the hoot of the owl, the rustle of leaves on the trees, and other sounds they didn't quite understand; echoing through the dark near stillness of their new world.

Author's Note:

You may note that the McTreggles had chosen to spend their first full night darks asleep in their new home, and not roam out and about as gnomes and elves usually do.

From their first night dark in Bluewater Wood as gnelfs, Duncan and Isabella had made a decision. *'Night dark was for sleeping, and light-day was for roaming'*, and it was a decision that would be copied by all gnelfs who chose to live above ground in the new gnelf world of Bluewater Wood.

The McTreggles had been banished from the gnome and elf world of Blackwaterfoot Forest, so it was not all that surprising that they would make a joint decision that would make them and their followers forever different.

Looking at each other in the dark interior of their new home, (gnelfs can see in the dark) the only gnelfs to be in the wood on that first night dark began to consider their new life.

While the other little folk and creatures of the wood all knew that something was happening, something that would change Bluewater Wood forever; they went about their business in a kinder and happier way. The influence of the new immigrants was spreading.

An samhradh math.

Chapter 26
The Good Summer

The time of summer season in Bluewater Wood is just as it is in many other places in Scotland, with it being the best time of season of all, and with the natural life of the wood at its best, everything seemed to be perfect, so perfect that even a shower of rain made no mind to those who call Bluewater Wood their home world. However, of course, there can be exceptions, can't there?

"Duncan!"

Mistress McTreggle's voice echoed inward from the open doorway of her new home, and the one word seemed to make its way easily to Mister McTreggle, down to the bedroom area three floors down from the doorway.

The name *Duncan* echoed through rooms and down the steps; the same Mister McTreggle had carved out of the solid wood interior of Big Oak. Then, ever so faintly, the name-word bounced off the polished wall of the bedroom, and then, insisted its way under the soft wool blanket that the *Dunky* in question was sleeping under.

"Yesssss?" a mumbled and muffled reply from the sleeping Duncan, to be then followed by the silence of a long pause, a real luxury of a pause from the same Mr Duncan McTreggle.

Then:

"Duncan McTreggle, dunna you *yessssss* me in that tone of voice, it…It isn't nice, not nice at all." The words spoken by Mistress McTreggle had not echoed this time, they had come from a position that the eye closed and head buried Duncan estimated to be at or near the bottom of the steps in the very room wherein he lay a slumbering, or trying to.

And then: Realisation for our Mister McTreggle.

The tired and weary Duncan sat up, swung his legs out from under the warm snugness of his blanket and allowed his bare feet to touch the hard cold floor; just at the very moment he chose to speak to his wife, "Yessssss, Izzy?"

The stretched-out *yes* was a verbal reaction to the sudden cooling of his nice warm feet on the cold floor of the bedroom and not an ill-tempered rude response from a sleepy gnelf.

But Mistress McTreggle wasn't ready to understand the association between warm feet and cold floor. "Duncan McTreggle! Don't you be rude. What have I said about you *yessssing* me? Do you really have to?"

Duncan was going to explain, but experience had educated him to make an effort to be extra polite and as nice as possible instead. "Sorry, Izzy, it won't happen again, promise."

It was an honest statement, he really was sorry, and Isabella responded in a like manner, "Oh, piffle, paffle, puffle, wuffle, suffle…Oh, it's okay, I'm just a bit miffed with the weather. It's raining again."

Her way of speaking carried the tone of one, who had been looking forward to another sunny summer-time day in Bluewater Wood, but she had learned to understand that a wet wood could be a bit less pleasant than a nice warm, dry and sunny one. *Unless you are into minnow-tickling.*

The cold-footed gnelf by the bed tried to console his wife, "Oh, I'm sorry for you, Isabella. You were so looking forward to a picnic meal today, weren't you?" Duncan's words of comfort did go a little way towards making his wife feel a bit better, but then, when he seemed to make a quick recovery from his slumbering attitude and reach for his boots, Mrs McTreggle became a wee bit suspicious.

"You are sorry for me, aren't you, Duncan?" She used her tinkly voice as she continued, "That's really nice of you my husband, you can be so kind."

Mr McTreggle bent down to fasten his boot laces, thinking how the rain would have *sweetened* the water in the stream, making it more than likely that the minnows would come to the side of the waterway to feed.

Could be a good minnow-tickling day-morning, then his thoughts were brought to a halt by a few words spoken in a tinkly sort of way.

"You are really kind when you want to be, eh, Dunky? And I know you will be a good and kind daddy to the baby we will soon be having. And seeing that it is raining, it's just the day to make a start on the baby's room, eh? What do you say we get on with it, Dunky?"

Author's Note:

Whenever his wife used that tinkly way of talking, Duncan always seemed to find himself suffering all kinds of mixed-up feelings, and try as he might, he knew that there would be no way he would be meeting with the minnows on that particular light-day morning.

Nasty rain, Duncan thought.

Realising that he would not be going minnow-tickling made him cringe, but then the thought of a baby being on its way stopped him feeling sorry for himself, and forgetting all about minnows and tickling he laughed with Isabella as they prepared to make a start on what would be their first child's room.

Taking great care so as not to harm too much of the living and growing wood inside Big Oak, Duncan began to carve his way down the big tree's interior, to a level below their bedroom, a fourth level, to where they planned to carve out a room for the first gnelf child to be born in Bluewater Wood.

The thought of his wife and their first baby made Duncan proud of each chip of wood he managed to remove with his tiny knife, and proud of how each one was another step through his and Isabella's life together. Moreover, when he paused for a few flicks of time, he let the thoughts run through his mind; of how he was so lucky to have such a wonderful wife, and that they would soon be having a wonderful baby gnelf to love. Duncan McTreggle realised that it didn't get much better.

I tha ar leanabh air an t-slighe

160

Chapter 27
Our Baby Is on the Way!

Duncan was being watched by his wife Isabella, the *First Lady Gnelf of Bluewater Wood*, a lady who knew her own mind, and a lady who wasn't willing to stand for second best in anything, and that included effort.

"Come on, Dunky! Stop your daydreaming and get on with it, will you!"

It was a short sentence, but it was one that seemed to work a kind of magic, and when Isabella looked at her husband again a few flicks of time later, his knife was just a blur in his hand. It seemed as though he was sinking into the hole he was making, as he cut and chopped away at the wood of Big Oak like a rabbit digging in sand.

Seeing that all seemed to be right on the baby-room-making front, Isabella decided not to disturb her husband too much. He seemed to be getting on famously, and she contented herself by watching from a back seat position as it were, just for a flick of time or two, and then, as she made her way back up to their own bedroom, she sang a little ditty to herself.

"Diddly, doddly, duddly, who is big and bold?

Doddly, diddly, daddly, who is to be told?

Daddly, duddly, diddly, who is—"

She did not get any further with her ditty. "*DUNCAN! DUNCAN! DUNCAN!*"

Isabella's shouting of her husband's name echoed out through the doorway in the side of Big Oak, and out to the quiet of the damp wood, with every creature within hearing distance stopping whatever it was they were doing, to listen.

With his head deep down in the hole inside Big Oak that would be the stepway to their new baby's room, Duncan did hear his wife shouting his name, but only in a muffled sort of way. It was as if he was dreaming a dream, and his wife was a long way off shouting at him for some reason—to come for his tea meal perhaps.

"*Duncan McTreggle!*"

...Just a wee pause...

No, it was not anything to do with him going for a tea meal, he was almost sure of that, but...There it was again, and much louder, "DUNCAN!" And a lot closer.

Then, he could feel the toe of his wife's boot pushing and poking on his rear end.

He squiggled, wriggled, and squiggled some more, with each squiggle and wriggle accompanied by a *whoo* and a *haaa*, and then, the wood carving gnelf came out of his wood-carved hole and into the fourth-floor room, he and Isabella's bedroom.

Blinking his eyes and rubbing his stomach—he had dust in his eyes, and he had caught his rumbly stomach on a bit of rough wood: Duncan looked around for his wife.

Isabella had managed to sit herself down on the wooden couch that they had set down under the window hole of their bedroom. She was leaning back and holding her swollen tummy...He knew even before she said it.

"Duncan! Ooh, Duncan, it's our baby. What shall we do? Our baby is on the way!"

Baby-time is normally a lady thing in all forms of life: human, animal, gnome, elf, or gnelf. And, of course, at this particular baby-time, there was at least, one lady gnelf present in that small room hidden inside Big Oak, the mother-to-be herself, but that, my dear friend, was it.

Author's Note:

Now don't you go thinking that one lady gnelf should be enough, that would not be nice of you at all, would it now?

It would be much nicer if you were to be thinking along the same sort of thoughts that the gnelf father-to-be was stimulating himself with, the more I listen the better.

The father-to-be remained calm. "Don't you be an upsetting, my dear. Don't you bother yourself now. I will sort things out. Don't you bother none! It will be just fine. Don't you bother."

Gnelfs don't normally worry, but I suppose there are times when they do fret just a wee bit, and on this occasion, Duncan's face must have gone through every expression known to gnome, elf or gnelf, as his mouth gave forth with a constant stream of *don't bother* and the like, kidding himself that he was equal to the task.

Then the little chap had to be honest and allow the true sense of panic he was feeling to come to the surface.

"I know…I know…I'll—"

The *uncomfort* began to surge through him, welling up through his short chubby body, along his arms, and then to the very tips of his fingers.

"I'll—"

It was painful for his wife to see it. How much more could she put up with? How much more *faffing about* could she be expected to stand?

Not more than two flicks of time then, "Duncan!" she tried to shout over the pain and discomfort she was suffering through and through her whole gnelf self. (*Say those last three words quickly*).

Then, as if by some magical force of *proper*, she calmly realised that if she could hold herself in check for a few flicks of time, and use her tinkly voice, all would be well.

"Duncan, it's okay…Just go quickly and fetch Ben Old, he will know what is best to do. Go! Be quick!"

Isabella's soft bell-like voice had the right effect, and Duncan seemed to calm down enough to gather whatever sense of responsibility he could muster, to turn his common sense into something of a determined effort. It was a mustering of logic that he expressed in a calm and near tinkly voice that was not unlike the one his dear wife Isabella had just used.

"Yes, okay, my Beloved. You're right. Ben Old will help us, and he will know what to do, won't he?"

Isabella ignored her painful discomfort and smiled at her loving and caring, but slightly confused husband, hoping upon hope that he would be able to make his way through the soggy wet woodland to Ben Old's cottage, and that the two of them would then make it back to Big Oak in time.

…Just another wee pause—who knows, it might help the situation…

163

Author's Note:

I admit that it is easy for me to relate to this part of Duncan's story, and I hope it is just as easy for you to read my words. But for poor little Isabella to sit there in Big Oak, alone in the middle and silence of a rain-drenched wood, knowing that she would not be capable of climbing up the steps to the door if the need arose, and hearing nothing but the pittling *and* pattling *of the rain…It must have been very difficult for her indeed.*

Not many flicks of time after Duncan left Big Oak to go and find Ben Old, a brown clad-winged, tiny fairy lady fluttered up the side of Big Oak and entered the doorway into the McTreggle's new home.

"Hello, Mrs McTreggle, *Isabella*, don't you worry now, don't you be afraid, I'm here to help you—"

Isabella did not really know what to say, but she interrupted the first visitor to her new home by asking, "Who are you? Where did you come from?"

The fairy lady smiled nicely and said, "My name is Jillyver, and I'm a Woodens. I live just round the corner from you, under the holly bush…We knew you were coming to live hereabouts. Mr Badger told us."

Isabella relaxed a wee bit and welcomed her visitor, "Oh, do come in Jillyver, it's not much of a home yet, but you are welcome to…Ooh!"

Author's Note:

Uncomfort*? Where's that word from I wonder.*

Jillyver settled by Isabella and the two of them waited for the event to take place; for the baby to arrive, with Mrs Woodens the fairy making sure that the gnelf lady was comfortable.

When Ben Old heard what the soaking-wet Duncan had to say, the old woodsman knew exactly what to do. He knew how important it was for someone to be with the mother-to-be, and regardless of his old and wobbly legs, he practically flew through the damp and dripping wood, using every shortcut he could remember.

Paying no heed to the brambles and long straggly thin branches that whipped at his face and body as he plunged and forced his way forward, leaving Duncan to keep up as best he could—and he did keep up.

Within what seemed to have been just a few flicks of time, Ben Old was sitting on a thick wet branch on Big Oak, with his face close up to the open doorway of the McTreggle home.

Jillyver had managed to help Isabella to lie down on the grass-filled mattress they had dragged from the bed; with, perhaps, a wee bit of magic. She placed it on the floor by the window after Isabella had said that she wanted to give birth in the normal way of an elf—and now gnelf, on a bed of grass.

Ben Old was astonished, not only had he met a couple of gnelfs, but he now could also see another little folk-person; a folk-person with wings who was doing all that was required, and one who looked to be totally sure of what she was doing.

The old woodsman climbed back down to the ground, to where Duncan was waiting all in a tether. "It's alright, Duncan, your wife is fine, someone is taking care of her."

Then, he said something to himself as he wiped some of the rain off his shoulders, "I can't believe it…How many little folk are there in this wood o' mine? I have lived here all my life an' never seen hide nor hair of 'em, and now, it's as though they're coming out o' the trees all around me!"

Duncan was a wee bit mystified, and his thoughts began to whiz a bit. *What other little folk? Who is it that is looking after Isabella? Is Isabella all right? How is the baby?*

Then, they heard it, the cry of a newborn gnelf baby, the first to be born in the new world of Bluewater Wood, and Duncan lost all interest in questions.

Isabella was magnificent, and he couldn't have been more proud of his lovely wife, and of their new baby boy, and the gentle Ben Old was filled with a sense of pride himself. And then, believe it or not, the rain stopped, and the sun smiled its glimmering light off the wet leaves to reflect into that tiny room in Big Oak.

Both Duncan and Jillyver made it clear that mother and baby would have to stay in the dry and warm comfort of their room in Big Oak, for at least two light days.

Proud father Mister McTreggle made sure that his wife and son should want for nothing, and that meant that they were safe and dry, even if the mother complained that he was busy being *The Elder* again.

Of course, Duncan thanked Fairy Aunt Jillyver Woodens and Uncle Ben Old for their help and made it clear that they and her family in Jillyver's case, should come around and have a meal with them as soon as Isabella and the baby were able to be out of bed.

The Fairy Woodens lady accepted the invitation and said that if Duncan and Isabella didn't mind she would be popping around every morning; to see the mother and baby, and Ben Old said he would be happy to share a meal with them anytime.

Author's Note:

It should be understood, I suppose, but I want to say it anyway. The first-born of the new McTreggle family, Firbbal McTreggle, became the most important gnelf in Bluewater Wood, and to his Uncle Ben Old, *the tiny gnelf boy was like a breath of fresh air.*

The old woodsman had never known how it could feel to be an uncle, until then, and he was full to the brim with pride and loving understanding, and the old man's affection for his little nephew *was plain to see, and so was the fondness that was soon returned in full.*

A 'fas agus dol seachad air uine.

Chapter 28
Growing and Passing Time

Time passes, flick-by-flick and year by year as it always does, and Mr and Mrs McTreggle watched their son grow, and grow fast, as they and the Fairy Woodens became firm friends and neighbours.

In the McTreggle home, young Firbbal McTreggle grew stronger with the passing of each light-day, guided by a loving mother and father, watched over by a loving and caring uncle, and loved by a caring Auntie Fairy Jillyver. And by the time the young gnelf's baby sister Pebbal came on the scene, Firbbal had become shoulder-to-shoulder tall with his father.

"Dad?" Firbbal asked the question while he moved a twig from the grassy carpet near their home with his booted foot.

His dad answered as he picked up the twig and threw it into a nearby bush, "Yes, son?"

"Dad?"

"Yes, Firbby?"

"Dad, do you think—"

"Do I think what?"

Firbby paused before continuing, while his dad began to wonder if the young gnelf had picked up his mother's habit of asking question-questions.

"Dad? Do you think it would be right for me to go and stay with Uncle Ben Old? I am 10 years now, you know. I will be grown up next birthday time?" After pausing for a flick of time or two, and before his not-too-surprised dad could answer, Firbby continued, "I know he wouldn't mind. He is my uncle, you know!"

Duncan knew that Firbby wanted to do the right thing for all of them, but it was only right and proper that his son should seek the blessing of his mother before expecting his dad to be *The Elder* and decide.

He placed a hand on his son's strong shoulder. "Go talk with your mother, Firbby, tell her that you have told me and that I don't say no." With his hand still on his son's shoulder,

Duncan thought for a flick of time or two and then spoke calmly to his son, "Firbby, I have never said this to you before, but I am proud of you. And so is your mother, and so will your sister Pebbal when she gets to be older. And so are Uncle Ben Old and Auntie Fairy Jillyver."

He let go of his son's shoulder and then spoke with a bit of a lump in his throat, "Remember your family at Big Oak, and come and see us often. Often, do you hear?"

Isabella did not like the thought of her son leaving them, but she knew that it was just one of those things that every family deals with, and it was one of those things that every son and daughter deal with at some time.

Holding back the tears as best she could, with baby Pebbal cradled in her arms, Isabella accepted the kiss her son gave her on the side of her bright red face, with the mum knowing that he must have tasted the salt of her tears. Then she told him to stay proud of being a gnelf, and a member of the McTreggle family, the first gnelf family of Bluewater Wood.

Then, with a smile on her lips, and a moist brightness in her eyes, she said, "Now, look here my young handsome gnelf, you bring a good lady gnelf to see us before long. Don't you be wasting time, find yourself a lovely lady gnelf and be my boy...Yes?"

Firbby could see the watery glint of tears in his mother's eyes, and not wishing to prolong things, he answered her last question calmly and confidently, in a way that seemed to calm her, "Don't you be a worryin', Mum, before you know it you'll be a happy grandma-gnelf."

Isabella wasn't too sure of what her son had just said, she didn't feel old enough to be a grandma-gnelf, and anyway, grandma-gnelfs don't curse, and Isabella McTreggle did, it would seem, "Wiffle, wuffle, ruffle, piffle, paffle, puffle."

Smiling to himself, Firbby climbed up the steps to the doorway on the side of Big Oak, and then, just before he moved outside, he turned to take a look at his mother and sister. "See you soon, Mum. Look after Dad and Pebbal, won't you?"

Taking one last look through the doorway from outside, he could see that mother and daughter were both crying, with mum cupping little Pebbal's head in her hand, and holding the tiny pink face to her own red cheek as she rocked backwards and forwards while twisting her long, frocked body in a sort of gentle slow-moving dance.

Author's Note:

Walking into a strange room can be a little confusing, but walking into a strange new world can be a lot more than that, even for a gnelf.

'Daoine ura.'

Chapter 29
Newcomers

Being the only family of gnelfs to live in the leafy new world of Bluewater Wood on the Sannox Estate, on the Isle of Leodhais, was good for the McTreggles.

They had the freedom to meet with many of the Fairy Woodens that lived in the trees and bushes of the wood, and to roam here and there just as they wished. They could enjoy the many different areas inside the fence that had been erected around the woodland many years ago in the past—possibly in an attempt to keep it private when it was part of the Sannox Estate.

But despite this freedom to roam Duncan and Isabella had always agreed; along with the Fairy Woodens, that there was more than enough room for other family groups in their new world. They had often discussed how they might seek out other gnomes or elfs who would care to join with them and live above ground in freedom—to become gnelfs in fact.

...However, there was a problem...

There was the problem of the ban imposed on them by *the Elders of Blackwaterfoot Forest*, which meant that they could never return to that place. So, how could they hope to talk with other gnomes and elfs, and tell them, if they were not free to go to them, to visit and chat?

They knew that they must obey the ban, so as to avoid bringing more disgrace on their family members still living in Blackwaterfoot Forest. But if they couldn't get to the gnomes and elves of the forest, how were they going to attract more immigrants? Maybe, the Fairy Woodens could help?

'S e sràid aon-rathad a th'ann
shesh srah-j eun rah-at uh ha-oon
It's a one-way street.

Chapter 30
The New Immigrants

Author's Note:

This chapter deals with the next family to arrive in the New World of Bluewater Wood, and how it came about that Firbby should meet with a special lady gnelf,

Because the events happened 10 time-years after the McTreggles had made their home in Bluewater Wood, it may take the story a little step backwards—but then, that's how Duncan related this part of the story to me.

…

Droggden Miggle, a gnome of Blackwaterfoot Forest, had been married to his elf wife Brinter for nearly 10 time-years when they had heard about Duncan and Isabella McTreggle's banishment from the forest, it had made them think and think some more. Then, with both of them being *The Elder*, they made a decision, and one that would change their lives forever.

Believing that they would be better off if they went away from what was the sometimes-unbearable control of the gnome and elf Elders, Droggden and Brinter made the decision to leave Blackwaterfoot Forest; to emigrate, to give themselves and their daughter Meggal a better chance of a real happy life.

They made their minds up, and without telling anyone, apart from Meggal; who was going with them anyway, Mister and Mistress Miggle planned their escape.

They planned to travel along the way they reckoned to be the one taken by the McTreggles some 10 time-years before; a plan they had worked out after Droggden had taken lots of time to sort things out in his mind, and then to prepare himself and his wife Brinter; and daughter Meggal, for the journey. He would be leaving nothing to chance.

Author's Note:
  Do gnelfs take chances?

When Droggden and Brinter had first thought of the plan to emigrate, Droggden had made some discreet enquiries. He even went so far as to chat here and there with one or two of those who had been in the party that had helped to escort Duncan and Isabella McTreggle when they had been made to leave Blackwaterfoot Forest.

However, Droggden did not stop there; he found and chatted to some of those who had known of someone who had been involved in the decision to banish the McTreggle couple in the first place. He even went as far as having a word very secretly with other members of the old McTreggle family who still lived in the forest.

But, best of all, he met and chatted with a certain Mister Dallan Woodens, a brown clad little fairy folk gentleman he had met quite by accident by the caves near the forest, and it was that gentleman who had told Droggden that a warm welcome would be there if he and his family ever came to Bluewater Wood. Then, somewhat mysteriously, the little fairy folk gentleman went on his way without telling Droggden how to get to Bluewater Wood.

However, all in all, Droggden did manage to gain some information, although he had to admit that some of it was just tittle-tattle, but even so, a good part of it was useful in many ways.

Everything was made ready, including the all-important map, and then, just at the beginning of one light-day, the gnome/elf family group consisting of Mister Droggden Miggle, Mistress Brinter Miggle, and Miss Meggal Miggle, calmly and secretly left their home in Blackwaterfoot Forest, knowing that there was no turning back—they were leaving for good. They were emigrating to become gnelfs.

By choosing to start their journey at the beginning of light-day, when the Blackwaterfoot Forest gnomes and elves would be retiring to their homes and beds underground, the Miggles were able to avoid the possibility of umpteen niggling questions. Then there would have been questions that could have meant more questions, and possibly a long delay that could turn into a reason for not going at all.

Droggden strode forward in the ever-brightening light-day, feeling a sweet sense of freedom that got sweeter with each stride he made. However, he sensibly stuck to the plan and stayed in the shade of the hedgerows where possible.

It's good sense to be out of the forest, and free, he thought, *but there's no sense in being foolish.*

...Float-walking...?

With the Miggles not having ever practised the art of float-walking, *they had always left it to the more elderly gnomes and elves,* they had to struggle along as best they could, just as Duncan and Isabella had done at first, and they eventually arrived at the Lochranza ferry port.

Then, just as the McTreggle couple had done, Droggden and his wife and daughter came across a certain collie named Coyrie, who talked with them in a kind and mumbling sort of way—she had become an old collie dog since she had helped the others, the McTreggles.

"What have we got here, then?" The old collie paused in order to ease her aching bones a wee bit, and to scratch her side with the claws of one of her back feet, while she looked carefully at the Miggles.

Then, her back foot went down with a thump, and she began to talk again, "It's not so long back when I met up with some of your sort." She paused to think for a flick of time or two. "Ooh, I don't know. It might have been a bit more than not so long back...Yes, a bit more."

She paused again and made as if to have another scratch, but she didn't, and the foot she was about to use went down with another thump. "Let me think, it wer'...Well! No mind." Her back foot came up again, and she scratched for all she was worth, allowing bits of her fur and her old dog smell to drift towards and around the Miggles.

Mr and Mistress Miggle and daughter put their hands to their noses and mouths and turned their heads away; the smell of the old dog was strong.

Droggden braced himself by holding his breath for as long as he could, to ask a question through gritted teeth in a half-closed mouth, "Can I ask you—"

Coyrie interrupted, suddenly remembering that she should have introduced herself earlier, "Oh, my name is Coyrie the collie, and I helped some little folk like you some time ago, yes, it was some time ago…I know it was because I am finding it hard to remember it."

Droggden nodded his head in an understanding fashion. "Yes, I know Mrs Coyrie, but do you think…Would you know if we are on the right track for the Isle of Leodhais?"

Coyrie snuffled and spluttered importantly in a kindly sort of way, with one eye shut. "Oh, I suppose as I should tell you," she spoke softly, so softly that Droggden could hardly hear what the old dog said. "But I should warn you, it's easy to get lost.

"If you will take my advice, it would be better if you wait here while I have my sleep-time, I get tired so easily nowadays…I'll not be long." She yawned and looked at Droggden with her right eye, the one that was not so tired as the other. "What do you say then? What do you say to that, eh?"

Droggden could not say anything, not straight off, he had to think about it while he took a few gasps of fresh air, turning away from the smelly old collie dog while he did so.

Too late!

Coyrie had one last scratch at her side and then scrambled and shuffled away up the road to the town of Lochranza, and then over a ditch and up the side of a grassy bank, to then push her way through a gap in the bottom of a hedge, and then she was gone.

"Well done Drog'! She might have been good for us. But now she's gone we will never know, will we?" Mistress Brinter Miggle was within a hare's breath *(or should that be a hair's breadth)* of being the almost same in a voice as a certain *ruffly* Mrs McTreggle; her way of speaking seems to carry the same sort of tinkly persuasion.

Brinter continued, "Now then, my dear Droggden, what's our next move, eh? Are we to follow this road of traffic, or should we wait in the hedge bottom for *old stinky?*"

However, Droggden had run out of his *organised ideas* a long way back, and the chance meeting with Mrs Coyrie had been a welcome *idea*. However, now the old smelly dog had departed, what next?

"Not to worry, it will be fine, you'll see," then, even as he spoke, he thought of something, and sitting himself down by simply leaning onto the root of a hedge plant in the bank of the ditch, and indicating that he would prefer his wife and daughter do the same.

Droggden spoke with a sense of authority on matters of a travelling nature, "It's simple, my dear wife and daughter, all we have to do is remember that water always flows down the hill, one drop after another."

"So?" his wife asked the only question that seemed the correct one to ask at the time, and she then repeated it. "So? That's what I've already said!"

The husband enjoyed the moment, a moment when he could be *The Elder* in a big way, and ignoring his wife's statement he carried on, "Well, my dear, if we follow this here ditch-dike within we are within." He paused for a think.

Author's Note:

I'm not sure what he meant by within we are within, *but then, he is a gnome-gnelf.*

He then completed his description of his new idea plan, "We have to cross the big water over to the other side, to what the humans call the Kintyre. I am sure we will find a way to do it on our own, yes I am sure of it."

Author's Note:

Oh, it is sad how gnomes, elfs, gnelfs, and humans, sometimes get it completely wrong. It is even sadder when the individual in question proclaims beforehand that he or she is certain beyond any shadow of a doubt that they will find the answer to the problem, in this case, the way forward. It was such a pity, Droggden Miggle had been doing fairly well up to the point when they had rested on the side of the ditch after talking with Coyrie.

I cannot prolong this notation anymore, so let it be enough for me to say that Droggden's idea, last gasp as it was, was totally and utterly wrong. In fact, he could not have been more wrong if he had tried.

After much struggling, and many pauses for rest, Droggden, Brinter, and daughter Meggal, eventually arrived near the ferry-point, right on the very edge of the water, and onto a shore of soft sand and shingle, with no idea of how they were to get to the ferry itself. The immigrant Mister Droggden was well and truly stuck.

With light-day still present, mother and daughter had relied entirely on the leader of their little family group of immigrants, followed his footsteps, and walked right to the water's edge with nowhere to go but back to where they had talked with Coyrie the collie.

Author's Note:

I suppose, it would be kind of me if I were to draw a veil over the events that followed, but I have a secret urge to be ever so slightly not so kind. Therefore, let Mrs Miggle have her say:

Mistress Miggle:
"You bucket brain of a gnome, you imbellical."

Author's Note:

Not sure what she meant there.

Mistress Miggle:
"You bit of a…You dented brained, beetle-headed blimber."

Author's Note:

Or what she meant there.

Mistress Miggle:
"You sludge footed, fettle headed, num-cum-cooper-dooper."

Author's Note:

No idea, what she was on about there either.

Then Mistress Miggle's voice calmed and dropped to a low mumbling "Wuffle, suffle, duffle," and so on.

Realising that he had taken a step too far, or maybe, even two or three steps too far, and become stuck on the muddy shore, Droggden tried to repair the damage to his *reputation* as leader.

Author's Note:

Reputation?

Lifting his right leg slowly and carefully, feeling the wild reed clinging to his bootless foot as he did so, he tried to turn round. But the other leg, which was still stuck in the mud up to the knee, refused to move with the rest of his body; with the sad result that Droggden Miggle groaned with pain and disappointment, and fell slowly and artistically backwards on the *sandy* beach.

"Aaaaah, splurt, splutter, and swuffle, swaffle, swuffle, swaffle, swiffle, and spaffle."

The struggling gnome/gnelf did his best to save himself, wriggling and squirming his face sideways in the muddy sand. Then, something must have got up one or both of his nostrils, with the effect that this nose-hole intake meant that the unfortunate Droggden took a huge intake of air through his mouth.

To be more precise, a mixture of air and grit, and then, just a few flicks of time later, he sneezed, "Aaaaah-choo."

Mistress Miggle was sure her husband's *leg-in-the-mud* had come out with a *plummmp*, and that he had floated at a good leg height above the beach just before he had sneezed. Furthermore, when he sneezed, he had shot three or four lengths of his body backwards; with his height above the beach remaining the same for the whole of the short journey as he seemed to float above the sand and mud.

Her husband's sudden burst of floating had made the lady blink with amazement, and turning to glance at their daughter, who had had the sense to stay out of the wet sand.

The bewildered Mistress Miggle gasped, "Did you see that?"

Sadly, for Droggden, when his wife turned back again to look in his direction, he had made his return to earth, still face down, and still on or in the soggy area of the beach. But this time he'd had the sense to keep his mouth and eyes tight shut, with his head held on one side.

Slowly opening his mouth and eyes, and keeping his body motionless, Droggden expressed his wonderment at having experienced his first *floating,* "Wha? Whaaa? Whaaa?" Then, he asked another question, "What?" He did not get an answer, so he tried again, "What happened?"

Although he had asked his questions with a mouth that still contained a fair amount of muddy boggy stuff. A young lady collie dog standing a little way back, where the ground was hard and dry just behind Meggal, had heard the questions maybe only faintly, but she had heard them.

She thought it proper to bark-shout an answer, "You have just float-walked! Well, you have just *float-something*. Now, all you have to do to get out of there is to do it again, and this time, try taking a good gulp of air and hold it in. You'll see, it'll be easy."

Mother, and daughter Miggle, turned to look at the owner of the voice giving the answer to Droggden's questioning, and they were surprised to see a younger version of Coyrie the collie.

…Meanwhile…

Droggden Miggle; out on the beach, thought *what the diddle* and breathed in slowly and deeply. Much to his surprise, his body began to lift away from the boggy bit of the beach. Then, with bits of wet sand dropping down from nearly every part of him, the gnome/gnelf began to wave his hands in a swimming motion.

To his great surprise, he began to travel in a floating way, moving steadily towards the dry ground at the top of the beach, while he continued to listen to the words of encouragement shouted by the new arrival on the scene. "Keep to the dryer parts if you can, that will make it easier. If you go over water you will fall back down," the young dog doing the shouting was Coyrie's young daughter Egin.

With all the Miggle family safely on dry ground, Egin introduced herself and accepted their thanks as they introduced themselves to her. She then went on to explain the way of float-walking, although she admitted she could not do it herself.

The Miggles listened to every word the young dog uttered, while at the same time, they marvelled at her handsome looks, and her youthful wisdom. Droggden mentally declared to himself that he would be asking the young lady dog some questions once he had got dry and warm again.

How come a collie dog knows about float-walking, she could be one of them, he thought.

"I am Coyrie's daughter Egin, and she told me that she had met with you, I thought I would take a walk and get some fresh air. And with it being a fine light-day, I thought I might take a look at the ferry—"

She paused for a flick of time or two and then continued, "When I arrived at the side of the beach by the road of traffic, I could sense that someone was in trouble, and I walked around to *your* side of the beach when I heard your voices."

Egin glanced at Mistress Miggle and daughter Meggal. "Not knowing who it could be, I decided to take a quick look before heading back home, and I did a fast float-walk across the sand, and arrived by your part of the beach just as Mr Miggle sneezed." She looked at Meggal and at her mum and dad. "You know the rest."

Daughter Meggal was amazed, and she felt the need to do a bit of questioning as she admired the young collie, "How did you learn to know about how to float-walk? How is it that—"

Mistress Miggle stepped in, "That's enough, Meggal. Let the young, lady collie take us somewhere safe first, and then, we can have a proper questioning time together."

She smiled at her daughter, took her hand, and then motioned to her husband and the young collie to carry on with the float-walking towards the ferry-point.

Happily, in a slow and careful manner, Egin guided her new friends around the soft part of the sandy beach to a spot where she knew they would be safe. A point near the town where she could bring her mum, so she could meet with them and help sort out a way for them to get across the water on the Lochranza to Claonaig ferry; and maybe help them on their way to Leodhais which she knew was a long way away.

…

It was some flicks of time later, and Coyrie was rested, and after crossing the road of traffic carefully with her daughter, she was very happy to meet another gnelf family.

As much as she leaned her head over to whisper to Droggden, she said, "It's right fine to meet you and your dear wife and daughter, right fine. Do you know there is another family?"

Droggden answered politely, "Oh yes, we know all about them."

Coyrie smiled her doggie smile and carried on, "Well, my little friend, they let me help them on the ferry, and they went on their way safely with a good friend of ours when they got to Claonaig on the Kintyre." The collie looked at the Miggles and sighed. "But I think we have a problem this time, my Dears. Yes, we have a problem."

Egin yapped a question of her own. "What problem would that be, Mother?"

Coyrie thought for a flick or two and then spoke calmly to the Egin and the Miggles without any trace of a barking sound, "Well, you see, when I helped the McTreggles, there were only two of them, and it was easy for me to carry them in a bag and onto and off the ferry…But now, now I am older and not so good at carrying, and there are three of you."

After some talking, the dogs and the Miggles came up with the answer. Coyrie would take Meggal Miggle, and Egin would take Mr and Mistress Miggle; each dog having a bag to carry their friends on and off the ferry. In this way, in a repeat of what Coyrie had done for the McTreggles, the Miggles made it to the Kintyre and met with a deer called Edera.

…

With the help of the children of those who had assisted the McTreggles, and with a lot of magic and luck, the Miggle family, eventually, made it to Leodhais and Bluewater Wood in Bluewater Glen.

Author's Note:

Life has so many mixes that to find one that matches is very difficult, but sometimes, circumstance can play a happy part in things.

Chapter 31
A New Beginning for the Miggles

Unfortunately, Droggden had another mishap involving a failure to float-walk over a muddy bank; he and his clothing became to some extent slime covered, and to some extent rather smelly.

Fortunately, the first person they met was Ben Old, who was sitting on a bench at the back of his cottage. After a first bit of surprise, the old man was more than willing to help the new immigrants. And it was not long before they were talking as if they had been friends for many, many flicks of time.

As they talked a figure of another gnelf float-walked onto the scene by Ben Old's cottage, and he introduced Firbby McTreggle to the Miggles.

Mistress Miggle looked at Firbby, with a wide smile, as she continued talking with Ben Old, but looking at Firbby as she spoke, "I might tell you, Ben Old, we have been following the *McTreggle Trail* from Blackwaterfoot Forest, all the way to here. We are at Bluewater Wood are we? We have made it, haven't we?"

Droggden took a chance, and interrupted his wife, gently, "I never thought it would be so easy to find the McTreggles." Then, contradicting himself, he asked a question, "Where are your family, Firbby?"

And then, Brinter spoke up again, not all that pleased with her husband's silly question, "Don't be daft, come on! Let's find somewhere to sleep, I'm tired. You can ask Mister McTreggle about his family when we have all had a rest. Anyway, you stink, and you look horrible with that coating of muddy slime. You should get cleaned up, and nicely so, before you dry out and set solid."

Taking heed of his wife's declaration, Droggden started to look around for somewhere to clean off the drying muddy slime in which he was covered.

...Oh, and then...

Ben Old came to the rescue. "I've got just the thing for you. Drog' is it? I have a full kit of a Highlander's outfit I made for one of me dolls. It's just about your size I would reckon, and you can borrow it if you like. You can let me have it back when you've washed and dried your own kit."

The old woodsman paused for a flick of time or two, and then smiling, he continued, "But if you like, you can keep it and burn your old stuff. How's that, eh?"

Not many flicks of time later, with Ben Old, Firbby, Brinter and Meggal chatting in comfort by the old woodsman's cottage fire, the tartan clad Droggden the *Highlander* Miggle strutted into their midst.

Is e latha fliuch a tha ann.
It is a wet day.

Author's Note:
His new tartan outfit was a complete change from his normal gnome/gnelf green. In fact, he was wearing the red tartan of the legendary Corloch Highlanders.

With his thumbs stuck behind a thick belt, and a flat bonnet on his head, complete with two feathers, he looked every centimetre, all 13 of them, a Corloch Highlander of Bluewater Wood.

The Miggles had arrived, in style.

Author's Note:
Before I continue with my story of the gnelfs, (most of which was told to me by the Elder Duncan McTreggle himself); with the others telling me of further happenings, there is something I would like to share with you if I may:

When I first met with Duncan to talk to, he was minnow-tickling in the Brook of Gilt, at a part of the brook where the water slips by in an easy, slow and gentle fashion.

It was early on a morning that looked to be promising a nice warm summer day in the Bluewater Glen in the north of the Isle of Leodhais; the promise as it were coming from the mist that was spreading blanket-like along Bluewater Glen.

I do not want to ramble on too much, but if I could just say—

I am getting old now, and I do not walk along the glen anymore, I just can't manage it, even though I would love to. But I am happy to say, I still see my little friends; they pop in from time to time to tell me this and that, and more often than not, they ask questions. Questions, I am happy to answer all day long, or all light-day *long as they call it.*

If you should ever come by yourself, I do hope that it will be on a nice warm sunny summer day, and I hope you can make it in the morning early, when the mist floats in and around Bluewater Wood and along the bottom of Bluewater Glen. Just sit awhile and look at the peaceful scene, and enjoy the thought that in that mist is the calm secret world of the gnelfs.

I am looking out of my window now as I write, looking through the drifting and lifting mist; and seeing the green leaves of the oak and ash trees that have been living there in peace for hundreds of years, ready and waiting to make homes for those little folk we know as gnelfs.

Gnog, gnog! Cò th' ann?
Grock, grock! coe ha-oon?
Knock, knock! Who's there?

Chapter 32
Moving On

Some long flicks of time after Firbby had left the family home at Big Oak.

On one fine light-day beginning, an excited voice signalled a change in the daily gentle mix of life around Big Oak, "Mum! Dad! Pebbal! Auntie Fairy Jillyver!" It was Firbby, shouting from somewhere amongst the trees and bushes in the area of Bottom Trail.

"Mum! Dad! Pebbal, Auntie Fairy Jillyver!" the sound of the young gnelf's shouting seemed to be closer.

It was.

Mum was busy preparing a meal in the kitchen, the room near the outside door of their home in Big Oak, with Aunt Fairy Jillyver helping her. *Dad* was between Big Oak and the stream, on his way back from a session of minnow-tickling practice. And Pebbal was talking to a squig (squirrel) in a nearby tree; the little gnelf girl and the squig both sitting on the same branch as they nattered on about this and that.

Author's Note:
I would have loved to have been there to listen to the squigs.

Mum popped her head out the open doorway and shouted excitedly, "Hello, Firbby."

Even though she could not see him, she could not help but shout to him, and she could not stop herself from becoming a wee bit excited as she wondered at the reason for his visit.

Isabella had not shouted all that loud herself, but she was sure Firbby would have heard her.

Then, in an effort to make sure he *had* heard, and not bothering to hide the excitement she could feel welling up inside her, she shouted as loud as she could as she brushed her hands on her apron. "We're up here Firbby!"

A little way down Bottom Trail, *dad* Duncan had listened to both his wife and son; their voices carrying through the quiet calmness of the wood as he carefully avoided slipping into a soggy bit of marsh.

Cocking his head to one side, he raised his own voice in a shout to his son, the words he shouted echoing off the tall trees around him, "Hi, Firbby. Good to hear you. I'll be with you in a flick or two."

Pebbal put a finger to her lips and tried to calm her friend the squig; the poor little creature had been frightened by all the shouting, and she whispered a *shush* to the animal as its whiskers twitched along with its long bushy tail.

Then it scampered off, running along the branch the two of them had been sitting on, and to then, seemingly fell down to the ground to scamper to another tree, where it climbed up onto a branch to sit twitching and titching to itself in a cursing sort of way.

Pebbal made no mind to the squig's antics. She knew it would be back later for another natter, and she calmly scrambled down to the ground and made her way to Big Oak, just a few trees away, to arrive there at about the same time as her father Duncan.

Mum and Dad, daughter Pebbal and Auntie Fairy Jillyver stood quietly together on the grass near Big Oak. The four of them were looking to where a holly bush curved over a bit, around 20 of Duncan's strides away; creating an archway of bent branches covered in prickly, dark green shiny leaves, an archway that was just high enough for a gnelf to pass under it.

Firbbal McTreggle, their *Firbby*, float-walked into view through the green archway, with his face wearing a huge smile as he gently dropped to a standstill directly under the dark green arch of the holly. He waved a hand to his gathered family and auntie standing by Big Oak. He then turned to signal to someone with the same hand, someone who had not yet come into view.

…

That particular someone was Meggal Miggle, a young *elf/gnelf* lady with such delicate beauty that the sight of her made Isabella's heart fill with pride, for the both of them.

The mother and the new young lady did not hesitate, and within a flick of time, the younger of the two float-walked her way across the green carpet of grass, and embraced Firbby's mother; with the two ladies laughing and cuddling as if they had known each other for years of time.

…Meanwhile…

Duncan had float-walked over to meet his son and grasp his hand, which he shook as if he meant to pull it off his arm.

Firbby laughed as he took hold of his dad's arm with his free hand. "It's okay, Dad, go steady, I've not told you yet!"

"You don't have to, son!" Duncan exclaimed. "Your mother is telling me," he motioned with a nod of his head in the direction of the happy lady gnelf and her new elf/gnelf friend, both of them crying.

Son and father looked at the ladies, and Duncan said, "I don't think there's any need for you to tell me, eh, Firbby?"

Firbby smiled to indicate that he did in fact understand the actions of his mother, and the words of his father, and he gladly accepted a kiss from a tearful Auntie Fairy Jillyver.

Even though the Miggles were in strange surroundings, they had a peaceful and comfortable night dark in Ben Old's kitchen/living room, with Ben Old's cat Clarry as company.

Author's Note:

When I had listened to Mrs Miggle telling her bit of the story, this was the first time she mentioned Clarry the Cat, and as she did so she spoke of Clarry in a comfortable and easy way.

With the calming night dark sounds of the woodland sort of creeping over the gate at the front of the cottage, and into the cottage itself, the tired and weary new family of Bluewater Wood went to sleep without any problem.

Then, it was light-day morning, the Miggle's first light-day proper in the new world of Bluewater Wood, and they were eager to go.

Breakfast was a quick nibbling affair of hawthorn leaves; with a radish each to keep their spirits up, and it wasn't long before they were all on the woodland side of the big wooden gate, with Firbby leading the way, and float-walking in a neat manner while looking in Meggal's direction at every opportunity.

He guided the new family along Middle Trail, with a few bangs, bumps and knocks *some of which belonged to Firbby* from some of the low-hanging branches, and the jutty-out stones; obstructions that young Firbby would have avoided normally. But, it must be said, things weren't all that normal for the young gnelf, with Meggal being there.

Eventually, a few knocks and bumps later, the new immigrant family of the Miggles arrived at Big Oak. And after much shaking of hands; slapping of backs, and arm-grasping cuddles, the McTreggle family and the Miggle family sat down to share in a welcome party meal in the McTreggle's kitchen in Big Oak.

The first family of Bluewater Wood: Auntie Fairy Jillyver and her husband Dallan were happy to welcome new settlers to their homes in the woody new world. And more than happy to know that the world of Bluewater Wood was going to be home to another gnelf family.

Author's Note:
The Miggles were given the title of Gnelfs *without anyone realising it, and they sort of drifted from being either gnome or elf in the natural way of things.*

With him, his wife and daughter being the new immigrants, Droggden Miggle did what he thought he should do, he made a speech, "Do you know folks, it's going to be good here, good for all of us. We can rest and be happy that our new world is going to be a good free world, with no meddling Elder Gnomes or Elder Elfs to bother or pester us with rules and regumalations." (*Good gnelf word that*)

Droggy stood up from the table to do his bit of speechifying, and before sitting down again he looked around to see if his effort was worthy of a reply.

It was, and it came from Mrs Isabella McTreggle, "You've got that right, Droggden, and, what's more, I might tell you that you have got a home here with us, until you can find a house tree for you and Brinter and Meggal. So, if you want to stay, you are more than welcome."

Isabella had not stood up to make her reply, but she had made things clear just the same; by offering shelter to the new family she had shown how generous and kind a gnelf family of Bluewater Wood can be.

Duncan practically beamed with pride at his wife's words, while at the same time, he cringed with the question in his mind of how could Big Oak be big enough. Big Oak home had been made for two and a couple of youngsters, which did mean; to him at least, that it was not a good idea to invite another family to stay and take up space; not a good idea.

Duncan felt the need to ask a question, "That's kind of you, Isabella, but isn't there a tree just a little way along Middle Trail that would make a fine home-tree?" The dumpy gnelf was smiling when he asked the question of his wife.

"What's that you say, Dunky?" Isabella gave her question/answer, fully aware of what her husband had said.

"A good idea, wouldn't you say, Izzy'?" Duncan was getting good at it, and his wife responded skilfully.

"Why do you say it's a good idea?"

Duncan was not going to give up that easily. "Don't you think a good idea on its own is the right thing for us?"

"Yes," his wife answered in agreement and paused. Then continued, "But without cleverness, how can it be a good idea?"

Fortunately, for everyone, including you and me, Auntie Fairy Jillyver Woodens twigged on to what was going on, and while smiling mainly for her own benefit, she added, "So, you think we should go take a look, eh?"

The others understood the move Auntie Fairy Jillyver had made, and why, and they were grateful that she had.

"Mum?" Meggal spoke her mother's title in a soft tinkly voice, but it was still a question, and the reply was short and to the point.

"No!" Mum had made sure that question time was over by answering her daughter's question with one short word. Snd in this way, she stopped any further need for questions from her daughter.

Meggal shrugged her shoulders and muttered something, "But I only—" Then she shrugged her shoulders again and declined to finish what she had been muttering.

Then, with a sigh, she leaned her head on Firbby's shoulder and ceased talking altogether.

The Miggles did move into the home-tree they called Middle Oak on that first day; finding on inspection that there were prepared nest holes where they could, at least, be sure of some shelter. Moreover, it wasn't many light days before they made a nice cosy home-tree home, for two of them that is, daughter

Meggal had to make do with a bundle of grass and weeds near the open and draughty doorway.

But things did improve slightly when with Ben Old's help, Droggden put a door on the entrance to their new home. However, Meggal still had a bundle-bed near the door.

"Mum?" it was Meggal asking a question and this time, Mother was prepared to listen. Whether she would answer the question was a different kettle of pebbles. *(Eh?)*

"Mum?" Meggal's question number two.

"Yes, my Meggal?" Mother's question-answer.

"Mum?" Meggal's third question.

"Yessss?" Mother's second question.

"Alright, Mum, there's no need to *sssss* to me. There's no need for that. I only want to know something." It would seem that Meggal had stopped asking questions or was her reply a question in disguise?

"What's that then, my Meggal?" Mum had calmed down enough to ask her question calmly and quietly, in the tinkly way lady gnelfs have when they want to sort things out once and for all.

Meggal took a deep breath and floated up a wee bit, then, realising she had accidentally put herself in the float-walk position, she let out her breath and dropped gently to the ground, and the nitty gritty.

"Mum! I've been thinking." She looked at her mother for a flick of time or two and then continued, "Mum, I've been thinking. You know Firbby and I are together now, don't you?"

Mother Miggle had been expecting this for a good long time. In fact, she had been waiting and hoping for *this*. It was what she and her husband had planned for, that's why there had been a bundle-bed by the door; a sure sign from the parents that it was time for the *child* to leave their home-tree.

Before *mum* could verbally react to what the daughter had just said, the daughter came out with the reason why they were having the conversation, "Well, Mum, I think it's time that Firbby and I get married, don't you think?"

Now, that was the sort of question that *Mum* Brinter did not mind at all. In fact, it was one she was more than happy to answer with a proper answer.

"Oh, Meggal, that's just grand. Your dad and I will be happy for you an' Firbby if that's what you both want—" her voice trailed off, and the tears began to flow, she couldn't help it, it was only natural, but she was quick to lift up the bottom corner of the front of her sleeveless jacket to dab away evidence of tearful moisture.

It would not show any indication of tearful sadness at the thought of her daughter leaving home.

"Oh yes, Mum! Oh, yes! It's definitely what we both want and thank you, thank you, thank you—" Now, it was Meggal's turn, and there was no shilly-shallying as she allowed her tears to flow freely. And within a few flicks of time, she was crying fit to burst, while laughing and dancing a jig-dance around her laughing and crying mother.

Brinter waited and allowed herself to enjoy the moment, and then her daughter ceased her dance-jigging about. Just when the mother was about to explain some of the things to do with her daughter and Firbby getting married, and husband and father Droggden appeared on the scene, pulling Ben Old's trolley-truck behind him.

"What's all the commotion then?" He had witnessed his daughter's jig dancing from up the trail. "What's this dancing and laughing about then, eh?"

Droggden stood just a few steps away from his wife and daughter, with the handle of the trolley-truck resting at the bottom of his back, his hands fisted around the top of the handle to push it to one side so he could lean on it; positioning it just under his belt at the bottom of his back.

Mother Miggle looked at Father Miggle, and at the pose he had adopted. "Aw! Give it up Drog', you look as if you are constipated, pulling a face like that and squeezing your side. It is only our daughter getting ready to get married. You should be proud and happy, not constipated!"

Meggal's jig-dance a few flicks of time earlier had been a bit on the lively side, but when Droggden heard the words about his daughter getting wed, being lively took on a new meaning.

He pushed the trolley-truck handle behind with one hand, and used the other hand to slap his raised thigh, to yell at the top of his voice, "*YODY, YODY, YODY, YODY, YODY!*"

It was a gnelf cry that had never been heard before, anywhere, but at that precise flick of time it was a cry that could be heard all over Bluewater Wood. And, it must be said, over parts of Bluewater Glen itself, including the bit where Ben Old's cottage stood in the shade of the leafy trees. The sound sort of came with the sunlight as it flickered through the branches and shimmered on the white-painted walls of the old building.

Ben Old had been thinking of taking a walk down to the Brook of Gilt, and he had just turned to close the door of his cottage when the *Yody, Yody, Yody* cry had echoed behind him in the woodland; the sound seeming as if to bounce off one tree and then another in a laughing sort of way.

"What the?" The old woodsman steadied himself on the door frame and turned to look towards the wood.

Then, smiling to himself for some reason he couldn't quite fathom, he sat down on the little wooden bench by the door, to wait in quiet contemplation as to what would happen next, in an old man sort of reaction.

Sometime later, perhaps, 20 of Ben Old's minutes, Firbby appeared; coming along Middle Trail waving his arms, and dancing a strolling jig-dance as he moved nearer to where Ben Old was waiting patiently in the sunlight.

He got up from his bench and moved towards the big gate to the wood, where the two of them met each other at the gate to Ben Old's garden, with Firbby shouting up from the woodland side of the gate, "Hello, Uncle Ben. I've got some great news to tell you!"

The old woodsman waited for Firbby to jump-climb to the top of the gate before speaking to him, in a whisper.

"My, we're in a bit of a state this light-day, aren't we?" He could see that the little gnelf was eager on eager to tell him something.

But, unusually so, the old man had suddenly gone a bit tired in a fainting sort of way, and needed to take a breath before listening to what his little friend had to say.

Then, he gasped out with a request, "Let's you an' me go an' sit down a bit Firbby, eh?"

Author's Note:

It is well known that most fairy folk can tell when someone is not well, and it is more than likely that Firbby sensed that it was more important for his old uncle to find a seat, than it was for him to go on about his news.

Once they were in the cottage, and after making sure his Uncle Ben Old was comfortable, Firbby told of his good news.

"It's a happy time-day for me, Uncle Ben, a happy time-day for all of us who live in Bluewater Wood." The little gnelf paused for a flick or two and then tried to stand tall as he continued, "I'm going to be wed!" Another pause. "I'm going to be Meggal's husband! Now what do you think of that, eh?"

The old woodsman didn't answer straight off. He was too full of emotion to speak, and he reached out to pat his little *nephew* on the shoulder with a finger, with the result that Firbby rocked back slightly, but didn't actually move away as the finger on Ben Old's right hand tapped him lightly on the shoulder.

"Do you know, Firbby, that's the best news I've had since I first met your mum and dad. It's the kind o' news I've been waiting for since I saw you an' Meggal together." The old woodsman bent over as far as he could safely do so and whispered to the happy little gnelf, "You'll make a fine husband and wife, bless yer both."

Author's Note:

Now, it has been said that old men do not cry, they just sort of snuffle and cough, and then, put a finger and thumb over their eyes and sneeze.

True to old man tradition, Ben Old snuffled and coughed, and then he put a finger and thumb over his eyes, and laughed!

Then, still laughing, he slapped his thigh, looked up at the sky, and yelled, "Yody! Yody! Yody!"

The sight and sound of Ben Old doing his yodelling made young Firbby step back a few paces. In fact, he was nearly knocked off his feet with the surprise.

Curled up on a cushion in the fireside chair, Clarry the Cat flicked the end of her tail somewhere close by her nose, opened her eyes to the slit position, and thought about her tea meal, her meal in the peace and quiet of the cottage. Clarry could not abide noise of any kind, and she always thought it best to ignore such a thing.

Outside just by the back door of the cottage, and underneath the canopy of a lilac tree, a conversation was taking place; a conversation that involved the old man and his little friend the gnelf, with the old man using the questioning way he had often heard the gnelfs use.

"Now then, Firbby, when can I see your bride-to-be? Is she goin' to come an' see me eh? What do you say?"

Author's Note:

I think the old chap was getting just a wee bit excited.

Ben Old's face left nothing to guess at, he was bursting with happiness for his little *nephew* of a gnelf. "Come on, Firbby, are you goin' to bring the wee lass to see us, to see me an' Clarry, afore you get married?"

Firbby was really eager to give his Uncle Ben an answer, but before he could do so there came another question from the old woodsman, "Can you both come an' have supper tonight? I'll get some nice radishes out the garden for the both of you!"

By making a statement straight after a question, the old man had broken the questioning custom, and by doing so he had given Firbby his chance.

"That will be fine, it'll be grand, Uncle Ben, we both like radishes as you would never think possible," Firbby tried to use the tinkly way of talking that gnelf ladies were good at, but he couldn't quite manage it. But the old man got the message just the same as the little gnelf continued, "I will be proud and happy to bring Meggal with me for a supper meal with you and Clarry...When we are married."

The old woodsman was put out by Firbby's delaying tactic, but he accepted that it must be a gnelf thing, and smiled down at Firbby, and watched the little gnelf turn and jump-climb over the garden gate, waving goodbye as he did so.

Author's Note:

The next part of the story was very difficult for me to write, but I had made a promise to my little friend Duncan.

As I have already mentioned, Meggal had told her mum and dad of her intention to be married, and Firbby had done the same by telling his family. However, sadly, the little gnelf and his new wife never had the chance to keep a promise to have a supper meal with their Uncle Ben Old, and I have to share with you a happy day that was also a sad one.

Cha tig an aois leatha fhèin

cha jeek un leh-a haen

Age doesn't come alone.

Chapter 33
Taken Away

The first wedding to be held in Bluewater Wood actually took place in the corner of a field of short, cropped grass just outside the wood; the grass kept that way by the chomping and chewing of Ben Old's sheep, all 10 of them. But they didn't chomp or chew the flowers.

Swaying at shoulder level to the gnelfs, the tall buttercups seemed to match nicely with the knee-high stumpy white and pink of the daisies; with the yellow tops of the buttercups swaying above the dancing mixture of grass and daisies as the gnelfs of Bluewater Wood float-walked their way to a wedding.

It was to be a simple sort of wedding, with the bride dressed naturally in a skirt of oak leaves, topped by a jacket of daffodil petals saved for the occasion. The whole ensemble was complimented by a hat made from the largest oak leaves that could be found, their ruddy brown colour matching her brown hair to perfection.

She was a beautiful lady gnelf, with a small baby squig in her left hand, with its tiny eyes sparkling and its bushy tail twitching, while in her right hand, she held a posy of daisies.

The groom was dressed in his smartest green trousers and jacket, with a round acorn-shaped green cloth hat on his head. In his hand, he held a twig of hawthorn with just three leaves on it.

Author's Note:
Duncan has never explained the reason for the hawthorn twig with three leaves.

...

The bride and groom sat on a bench made with two forked bits of twiggy branches from Big Oak as legs, and a straight piece of a twiggy branch from Middle Oak as the seat they were sitting on. Big Oak represented the McTreggle family and Middle Oak represented the Miggle family.

Although Ben Old attended the wedding, he had been asked to stay out of sight, in hiding under the leaf-filled branches of a nearby oak tree—the wedding corner of the field being close to the boundary fence of Bluebell Wood.

The McTreggles and the Miggles had wanted Ben Old to be amongst them when Firbby and Meggal married, but they had decided that a human at a gnelf wedding just would not be right; there were too many secrets at a wedding ceremony, and they had asked the old woodsman to be a bystander.

Ben Old was okay about it; he was fine he said, and he understood when Duncan had explained things to him. As a result, the old woodsman was seated on a grassy bank that supported a healthy growing oak tree. The strong trunk of which supported his back comfortably; an arrangement that Mother Nature had often provided throughout his long life.

However, on this occasion it was an extra special arrangement, and, sadly, the young tree would be even more special after the wedding ceremony.

The old woodman watched the two gnelfs he had come to know and love. Yes, he did love them, as if they were his own children.

Author's Note:
It is true to say that all the gnelfs and the Woodens were his children, he had adopted *all of them without even thinking about it.*

*It was…*the old man began to think about things as if prompted by some sense of spirit. *It was as if. No! It was special.*

The two young gnelfs getting married were special to him.

He could feel his old eyes watering, and when a robin perched on a twig near the old woodsman's shoulder, began to sing at the top of his little voice. The old man just let go and laughed as he cried. Again laughed and cried, and laughed and cried, and then, fell asleep. Just like that, Ben Old, the old woodsman, went to sleep—forever.

The wedding took place, and Firbbal and Meggal became Mr and Mrs McTreggle. It was the way the old woodsman would have wanted it, no messy, muddling, maudlin fuss, and just happy cheerful chatter around him as he went to sleep.

With my own heart still aching with the thought of the loss of Ben Old, I will write what Duncan told me.

In memory of Ben Old.

Present were Mister and Mistress McTreggle and daughter Mr and Mrs Miggle, with Mr Miggle in his Corloch Highlander outfit, and Firbby*, as Ben Old always called him, (as we do) and his new wife Meggal with Auntie Fairy Jillyver Woodens and Uncle Fairy Dallan Woodens helping.*

They all saw to it that a gathering of daisies was planted under the young oak tree that had given their old woodsman friend shelter at the wedding, making it a special place in the woodland that had been his world for over 80 human years, a world that was now the Gnelfs and Woodens.

They planted the daisies quietly, on a misty morning when there was not the slightest breath of wind. It was as if Mother Nature herself. And the trees and bushes of the wood, were staying silent and still in respectful memory of the old woodsman of Bluewater Wood.

The old man who had cared for them, and just as they had given him shelter or shade in his lifetime when needed, now one of those trees would be giving his memory shelter for many years to come.

To the memory of Uncle Ben Old.

Author's Note:

It had been a sad thing to do, but the little folk knew that they had to keep the old woodsman's memory—it was what they should do, and on that quiet morning, they had said their last goodbyes to an old and loving friend in a fitting manner.

A message from Duncan McTreggle:

If at some time in the future, you should visit Bluewater Wood on the Isle of Leodhais, when the sea mist is drifting in the hills, and you come across his old cottage, and discover the old woodsman's memory place. May I ask that you speak a greeting, and feel the quiet peace he knew.

I think it only right that we should respect the old man, and the little folk he loved, so, if you can, nice and easy does it, eh?

You can be sure you will be seen, so take care, and be happy as you think of the old woodsman and the gnelfs. Know that the old trees and woodland the old man had cared for are for us to enjoy, and know that the gnelfs who are watching you will continue to take care of the peaceful world of Bluewater Wood.

Author's Note:

I am sorry, if Ben Old's going away came as a bit of a shock, just as it was for me when I first heard the story, and so, it must have been for Duncan and his gnelfs, but I did not want to drag it out and tell you bit by bit if you know what I mean.

Before the wedding, and before they learned that Uncle Ben Old had been taken away; Firbby and Meggal had found an oak tree near Ben Old's cottage.

Old Oak, as they called it, was to be their new home, the third gnelf home in Bluewater Wood. And a fine home it made, the new Mrs Meggal McTreggle saw to that.

There were no second-rate shortcuts with Meggal, as far as she was concerned a home was a home to be proud of, no matter how humble.

…

Although Old Oak wasn't quite so wide and as tall as the home trees of their parents, even though it was probably older than Big Oak and Middle Oak.

Author's Note:
It was just the way it had grown, I suppose.

Firbby and Meggal worked hard to make the tree fit the needs of their new gnelf family of Bluewater Wood.

They made the steps inside narrower than usual, and the rooms were smaller than the Elder McTreggle and Miggle rooms. But somehow, in its smallness, Old Oak became a cosy *tree-cottage*. It even had a wooden bench disguised as a tree mushroom just outside the door.

Of course, things being as they are, it wasn't long before Firbby had to make another room in their tree-cottage for a new baby. And in the passing of time, Meggal gave birth to a son. Duncan and Isabella, the *First Gnelfs* of Bluewater Wood, became the happy Grandpa and Grandma McTreggle, along with Grandpa and Grandma Miggle.

It was some light days later when all the gnelfs gathered at Old Oak to be happy for the birth of Benddit.

Author's Note:
   I didn't choose the name Benddit.

And, as with most gatherings at that period of light-day fading, the assembled gnelfs settled down by a flame-fire to share the news, their thoughts, and memories.

Duncan McTreggle was the *natural* leading Elder Gnelf. Natural because he was the eldest now Ben Old had departed. Anyway, it was he, who began the chin-wag session by mentioning something he had witnessed the light-day before.

"I was round by Ben Old's cottage last light-day gone, *yesterday,* and I decided to have a look in his shed, going in through the door-in-a-door he made for us." He looked at Droggden at that point and then carried on, "I know he wouldn't have minded me tekkin' a peep, and what could you want to know?"

Author's Note:
   I think he meant, 'And what do you know?'

There was nothing there, not even a broken bit of stick-wood. Ben Old's shed was empty of all the toys and other things he said we could have!

The gnelfs were amazed, or *flimmed* as Duncan had put it. Never in their wildest notions had they thought that Ben Old's things would be taken, not in one go like that.

Firbby spoke up, "It isn't right you know. Uncle Ben wouldn't have done that, he wouldn't have let all things like that go away. And he'd have made sure that things were right for us first."

The young gnelf knew he had spoken out of turn, *over* Duncan-the-Elder, but he had to have his say. After all, he had known Ben Old, *Uncle Ben*, better than any of them.

Droggden and Duncan looked at each other between the flitting and slowly circling moths in the flame-fire's flickering light. They were *Elders*, and Firbby should not have spoken out of turn like he had done.

Duncan shrugged his shoulders, and Droggden tightened his lips in a smile and nodded to his fellow Elder. They let it go. After all, it was just the sort of rule thing that had made them leave Blackwaterfoot Forest in the first place.

Although Firbby was well aware of his error, he carried on regardless, "I'd say…I'd say I'd known Ben Old better'en most, he was my uncle…And my friend when I was making my way to be grown up…So, me and him, the two of us, were real good pals."

The little gnelf was talking in a stumbling sort of way, and nearly dropping his voice down to a mumbling way of talking in fact. It was clear to the others that he still missed the old woodsman, and talking about him had made him miss him more.

Meggal touched Firbby's hand, and he gulped in a few bits of air and lifted slightly in his crossed-legged position. Then, realising that he was rising to a float-sit, he sighed at his wife. And with the two of them looking at each other, he dropped back down to the grass-covered bit of ground he had just warmed up.

Isabella had been watching her son as he had made his speech, thinking as she watched as to how like his father he was; trying to be speechifying when his tongue was not in tune with his brain. She sighed and sank a bit lower to the ground, not because she thought she was at risk of floating away, but more because she knew that her son's heart was in the right place, a lot like his father.

Then she made it her turn to be *The Elder*, "We all know that Ben Old would not have left us without. We all know he would want us to have things. And this is what I think we should remember, Ben Old's things have been taken away— stolen. We don't know who it is that's taken 'em, and maybe, even it's not for us to know! So, I think, myself, that is where we should leave it."

The others nodded and mumbled their reluctant agreement, and Isabella's declaration was accepted.

Some flicks of time later, after the meeting had closed, Firbby was float-walking his piffling, puffling and waffling way home, with his wife Meggal by his side doing her best to help sort out his thoughts as they made their way through under leafy bushes and trees of Bluewater Wood.

Author's Note:

Firbby was upset, yes, but there is no way I can let him piffle and puffle his way out of the story: Do not be feared, Firbby will be back.

It was true about Ben Old's shed, it *had* been emptied, but and what was even more sad, so had his old cottage.

The only things of the old woodsman's to be left were the old wooden bench by the back door, and Clarry the Cat, and she had staked her claim to the old bench. When it was fine, she would curl herself under it to keep cool. When it was not so sunny she would curl under it to keep warm. When it was raining, she would curl under it to keep dry. Yes, without a doubt, it had become Clarry's bench.

Epilogue

It was so much like being transformed or transported into a different world as I wrote. I can assure you, I was not on my own, my little friends were always there with me, and telling me what happen next. Also, laughing with me when the occasion warranted it to be so, and crying with me when sadness had to be told and shared.

I could let things trot on as it were, and write more words, but I am going to stop here and let sweet Mother Nature take over until we meet again. Please, enjoy your time with the gnelfs and your future with sweet Mother Nature.

Leslie H. Harvey of Kimberley
Moran Taing

Dedication to My Family

There are many things and events that are told about in the history of writing, but the story of the adventures of the gnelfs is much more to me; they are the fulfilment of a life spent wishing for better for my own little family.

It is with hope and gentle love that I bequeath the words in this book to my lovely family.

Leslie H. Harvey of Kimberley. January 2023

A h-uile la sona dhuibh's gun la idir dona dhuibh
(Uh houluh lah sonnuh ghuh-eev skoon lah eejir donnuh
ghu-eev)
May all your days be happy ones.